The weather had cl[...]
stantly and without [...] her feet and ran on. [...] buzzing lights illuminated her like a moth to be stabbed on a pin.

She ran across the playing fields toward the village.

Snow blew in her face and obscured her vision.

For three steps she ran on top of the snow. Then her foot broke through the crust. She floundered up to her knees. The wind whistled around her head and through the three colors of her hair as if she were a barn roof.

She could not hear the giggle, but that was because the snow had become a storm, and the Atlantic Ocean was pounding and the wind shrieking. She came to the Singing Bridge, whose open iron fretwork made the car tires hum when they passed over. The iron was solid with ice. With each splash of the extremely high tide, another slick layer was added.

To get to Schooner Inne she had to cross the Singing Bridge.

It will sweep me away, thought Christina Romney. The sea will take me down into Candle Cove, and take me out with the tide. I will be frozen solid, like a maiden in an old poem: all ice. Even my heart and soul.

Exactly what the Shevvingtons want.

Caroline B. Cooney's
LOSING CHRISTINA trilogy:

Losing Christina 1: Fog
Losing Christina 2: Snow
Losing Christina 3: Fire

Other Caroline B. Cooney
paperbacks you will enjoy:

Flight 116 Is Down
The Terrorist
Mummy
Hush Little Baby
Emergency Room
Wanted!
Twins

LOSING CHRISTINA • 2

SNOW

ORIGINALLY TITLED
The Snow

CAROLINE B. COONEY

SCHOLASTIC INC.

New York Toronto London Auckland Sydney
Mexico City New Delhi Hong Kong Buenos Aires

ISBN 0-590-41640-5

12 11 10 9 8 7 6 5 4 3 2 1   1 2 3 4 5 6/0

Printed in U.S.A.   01

First Scholastic printing, February 1990
Originally titled *The Snow*

Chapter 1

Christina was alone in the cold mansion. January winds screamed off the Atlantic Ocean and tried to tug Schooner Inne off the cliffs and dash it onto the rocks far below. But Schooner Inne was very old, and the wind always lost the battle. Christina did not know why the Shevvingtons called it an "inne," because although there were eight beautiful guest rooms, there were never any guests. Just the five island children boarding on the mainland for the school year. And the children were stashed up on the cold, dark third floor, not in the sunny guest rooms. Criminals, thought Christina, have better housing than we do.

It was Saturday morning. Mr. and Mrs. Shevvington had taken Dolly shopping. They said Dolly needed new mittens. Christina knew it was true. But she felt so betrayed by Dolly, she wished Dolly's fingertips would freeze off instead. "You may not leave the house," Mrs. Shevvington had said to Christina. "Perhaps losing your weekend will teach you manners. What kind of example are you setting for Dolly? Accept your punishment as a thirteen-year-old should. If you leave the Inne, you will be confined to the house next weekend as well."

If Christina didn't have a Saturday and a Sunday to run and be free, to hold the sky and the wind — then she had nothing.

Dolly, hardly aware of Christina at all, let alone Christina's agony at being shut up in the house, had smiled lovingly at the Shevvingtons. How could Dolly adore them, with their eyes like mad dogs? wondered Christina. They were evil. But Dolly took their hands and skipped between them.

Schooner Inne was the highest building in the little Maine village. Christina could see all the way to Blueberry Hill, where children were sledding and skiing without her. Scarlet, gold, and green ski jackets dotted the snow like splotches of kindergarten paint spilled on white paper.

Anya came in. Christina had forgotten Anya was even alive, let alone at home. "Hi, Anya," said Christina dully. "How are you?"

"It's so cold in here, Chrissie."

Christina got her a sweater. Sometimes Anya even forgot how to dress. Then Christina took Anya into the kitchen, where it was warmer.

"Shall we watch TV?" said Christina hopelessly. Christina hated Saturday TV. "Shall we play a game? We could draw. Do you want me to get out the watercolors?"

Anya did not respond. She just stood there, thin and lost among the kitchen cabinets. All her romantic, fragile beauty was lost, as if she had put her own face somewhere and forgotten it.

After a while, Anya cleared the table of breakfast dishes. This winter Anya had ceased to be a teenager boarding for high school and had become a servant, good for laundry and dishes. She scraped every plate carefully, as if proud of this skill.

Christina could not bear seeing Anya and remembering what she had been. Anya used to love the telephone, giggling continually in her soft, happy chuckle to any of a dozen girlfriends or Blake. Anya used to read aloud from her English books. How well Anya could memorize! One night it would be a speech from *Hamlet*; Anya's slender body would take on a stern masculine pose while she flung her cloud of black hair like a cape. Another night her voice would deepen while in tragic tones she recited some grim poem about death in the trenches of World War I.

Christina stared out the window at the fallen snow. She loved snow. It softened the edges of the world and hid things.

"Do you remember Blake?" Anya said unexpectedly.

Do I remember Blake! Christina thought. I think I remember him better and more often than you. I'm glad you don't know the inside of my mind, where I pretend I'm on the dates you used to have with Blake, where I pretend he comes back to town . . . *and it's me he wants.*

It was wrong, this dream that had her heart. Christina remembered Blake standing on the rocks that bound the coast of Maine, framed against a blue sky and a black sea; that posture in which he looked like the owner, or even the conqueror, of any place he stood; those clothes, so casual, so expensive.

"Yes," said Christina. "I remember Blake."

"Is he alive?" asked Anya.

"Yes. He's at boarding school." Where Blake's parents had sent him after the fall from the cliff, which they had blamed on "those island girls," meaning Anya and Christina. The school Mr. and Mrs. Shevvington had suggested.

"Why doesn't he write to me?"

"I guess because you don't write to him. I'll help you write a letter to him," Christina offered. If Anya is thinking about real things again, Christina thought, if she does a school-type thing like writing a letter, maybe part of her will be real again. Maybe she just needs to get cranked up, like an engine in cold weather.

The big house shuddered as the tide hurtled into Candle Cove, slamming against the rocks on which Schooner Inne was built. Living with the tide was like living with a battalion of insane drummers, who every twelve hours beat on the foundations of the sea captain's house.

Christina had come to believe that the sea captain's wife, who threw herself over the cliff a hundred years before, had done it because she couldn't stand the noise anymore.

"What shall I say to Blake?" Anya asked.

" 'Dear Blake,' " dictated Christina, and to her delight Anya laughed.

"I could have thought of that myself," Anya said. *Dear Blake,* Anya wrote, and her handwriting looked like the old Anya, the Anya who should be graduating first in her class, come June. Not the Anya who had dropped out of high school and taken a job folding laundry at the laundromat.

In the cellar, somebody giggled.

Christina raised her head and listened again.

They were alone in the house, she and Anya. Dolly had gone with the Shevvingtons. Dolly's older brothers, Michael and Benjamin, had left hours before: Michael to basketball practice and Benjamin to his job pumping gas.

The giggle came again, low and taunting.

You can't find me, it said.

Christina's eyes frosted, as if it had snowed in her brain. Nobody giggled, she told herself. The sea can make any noise. It can whisper, chuckle, clap hands. This time its noise is a giggle. That's all.

"Chrissie, I'm still cold," said Anya sadly, as if there were no cure for this.

The cellar giggled again. Christina looked at Anya, but Anya had heard nothing. Last fall, when Anya had been so afraid of the sea, the tide, and even the poster on her bedroom wall — when Blake had been pushed off the cliff into the oncoming tide and would have drowned except for the tourist who happened by — last fall Christina had thought the Shevvingtons must have a partner. Somebody who was able to do these terrible things for them. But she had found no evidence, unless you counted the man in the wet suit she kept seeing everywhere, but who vanished whenever Christina tried to show him to people.

Christina pushed the thermostat up ten degrees, so Anya could toast along with her whole wheat bread. This was forbidden; it wasted fuel oil.

Who cares? Christina thought. The Shevvingtons get paid to have us here.

The furnace came on, rumbling. The house filled with deep shuddering noises from the sea, from the cellar. If there was still a giggle, it could not be heard over those growls and claps.

Maybe I'll go down and find out what's in the cellar, thought Christina Romney. It's probably just the tide and my imagination. That's what Michael and Benj would say. "You know what?" she said to Anya. "We've never explored the cellar. There are supposed to be passages from Candle Cove right up into this house. It's one of the legends, like the sea captain's bride falling to her death from the cupola. Let's see if we can find the passages." She located a flashlight on the shelf in the pantry and checked the batteries. Nice and strong. "You coming?" she said to Anya.

Anya stared at her in awe. "You're not afraid of anything, are you? I like being here with you." She smiled as trustingly as a kindergartner at Christina, who was thirteen to Anya's seventeen. "Listen to what I've written so far. *'Dear Blake. It's me, Anya. I miss you.'* How does that sound, Chrissie?"

It did not sound like a girl who had memorized Shakespeare.

Christina slid the bolt on the cellar door. She clung to her flashlight as if it were a grown-up. There is nothing down here, she told herself. "It's a great start, Anya." All fall her parents, her teachers and friends, and especially Michael and Benj had said to Christina, "Why do you blame the Shevvingtons for all the awful things that have happened? Why do you blame the Shevvingtons for Anya's mental collapse? The Shevvingtons are wonderful people trying their very hardest! You are making up all the connections you tell us about."

Anya said, "Shall I tell Blake we're having toast and tea, Christina?"

Christina turned the switch at the top of the splintery wooden stairs. The air was thick and dusty. "Yes, tell Blake that, Anya." She thought, We'll find out who's making what up. This giggle is the kind of thing the Shevvingtons would do to frighten one of us. The fall before, when Mr. Shevvington's eyes kept changing color, so that they were cold as gray steel one day and gaudy as bluebirds the next — why, it turned out to be as simple as two sets of contact lenses. And when the poster on the wall kept changing personality, so that Anya screamed whenever she looked at it — why, Mrs. Shevvington was just switching posters. Nobody would believe me. Grown-ups don't do things like that, everybody would tell me. Why, Mr. Shevvington is the best high school principal we've ever had, and Mrs. Shevvington is the most creative seventh-grade English teacher! *You're* the one making things up, Christina. That's what they would say.

I bet I'll find a tape with remote control down here, so they can turn on insane giggles and try to make us insane, too.

Down the stairs Christina went, flashing her light in the corners. She reached the bottom step and stared into the musty dark. A few old wooden sawhorses, a big wooden barrel, some discarded furniture, a broken table, old toolboxes, cans of paint. At some point in its long history the huge cellar had been divided into rooms. The doors of each room sagged on rusty hinges. One door had had a small glass pane in it once, but the glass was gone, and there was only a hole, as if a hand might inch through and touch Christina.

Don't think things like that, she ordered herself.

"There's a draft on my ankles, Chrissie," said Anya from the kitchen. Her voice was a thin, distant whine, like her life.

I'll follow the electric wires first, Christina thought. She looked up. A single lightbulb hung over the rickety treads. And no wires went anywhere; the only electricity stopped right at that bulb.

It could run on batteries, then, she thought.

Cautiously, Christina walked into the first room. Stone floor, stone walls, and cobwebs. She backed out and tried the next room. Stone floor, stone walls, and cobwebs.

The ocean in Candle Cove whiffled and whispered through the rocks.

She flashed her light in the corners. She flashed her light at the ceiling.

Up in the kitchen, Anya was muttering, "A draft. A draft. A draft." Christina heard Anya push back her chair and cross the room. Then slowly, as if not sure she knew how to do it, Anya shut the cellar door. The door closed with a thick wooden slap.

The light that had poured down from the kitchen vanished. The single bulb was weaker than Christina had realized. You could hardly even call it light; it was more like a fog.

From the depths of the cellar, Christina heard the flat, solid sound of a footstep.

Christina froze. It had not been her own foot. And Anya was too light.

Outdoors, muffled by the rock walls of the cellar, the Atlantic Ocean forced its way into Candle Cove. She swallowed. That's what it was, she told herself. Tide slapping rocks.

For a moment Christina wanted to flee back upstairs. But this was like a test, and Christina intended to pass. So she walked past the furnace, going deeper into the cellar.

She was tiptoeing. Why am I being quiet? she thought. Do I really think there's a creature down here I don't want to frighten? If there is anything down here, I definitely do want to frighten it.

Now the light from the single bulb was behind her. Her shadow was long, darkening her own path. With her flashlight, she split her own shadow in two. "Now one of you go in that room," she said to her two shadows, "and you there — you come with me." She giggled.

A deep, throaty voice giggled back.

Chapter 2

She did not scream.

The giggle sucked the air out of her lungs and kept it. Christina turned blue. Fighting her lungs, fighting the giggle, she tried to reach the steps. She stuck out her skinny little seventh-grade arms to defend herself.

The giggle thickened and grew deep until it became a groan. It was no tape. It was no trick. It lived; its inhuman noises reached for her like dead hands.

It was between her and kitchen door; the furnace, black and banging, hid it. She swung her flashlight, trying to catch the giggle in its beam. Her arm jerked with nerves and the light leaped around the cellar like fireworks, illuminating nothing. "Go away," Christina whispered.

Immediately: silence.

Christina and the giggle both ceased to breathe.

She circled, trying to keep her back safe, but not knowing where safety lay. She felt like a slow-motion ballerina. "Anya, open the door!" Christina whispered.

She passed the furnace, and nothing attacked.

She passed the sagging door of the empty room, and nothing touched her. "Anya!" she croaked.

The giggle began again, slithering off the stone walls like spiders.

Christina bolted up the cellar steps and grabbed the tiny handle. The handle spun, opening nothing. "Anya!" screamed Christina, pounding on the door with the flashlight. "Anya, you locked it! Open the door! Let me out! Anya!"

The foggy bulb above her head flickered.

"No!" screamed Christina. "Don't go out!"

It went out.

She turned, pressing her back against the kitchen door. "Please don't swim out of the dark," she prayed. "Please go away." She was whispering, as if she could not allow the rubbery giggle to hear her beg.

Christina touched her hair.

The strange hair that always protected her. The hair of three colors, with its streaks of silver and gold and chocolate brown. She felt that in the dark the charm of her extraordinary hair could not work; the rubbery giggle would not know that she was Christina of the Isle, with tri-colored hair.

She was afraid to aim her flashlight into the cellar.

What if she saw it? Its rubbery fingers ready to crush her against the kitchen door?

"Anya!" Christina kicked backward with her foot.

There was no sound in the cellar. No sound in the kitchen.

She could almost hear her own tears spilling down her thin cheeks. She was pressed so hard against the kitchen door, her own back ought to break through the solid wood like a tank.

But it didn't.

She was alone in the dark, in the cellar, with the giggle.

After a long, long time, she remembered her watch. It was digital and glowed in the dark. She stared at the tiny square numbers as they flickered away the seconds of time. Her skull filled with numbers and colons.

10:32:01.

10:32:02.

10:32:03.

At 11:17:45, Christina knew she was alone in the cellar. She did not know how she knew. But the giggle had gone. Evaporated like water? Or had it walked out another door? But there were no other doors.

She slumped against the kitchen door. She could cry no more; her face was so blotchy her eyes felt swollen shut. "Anya," she muttered once or twice, "please open the door."

How had this happened to her?

How had Christina, born on Burning Fog Isle, only daughter of the most wonderful parents in the world, ended sobbing and defeated in the cellar of a sea captain's house on the mainland?

Burning Fog Isle lay far out to sea. There were so few year-round residents that once the children finished the sixth grade, they were sent to board on the mainland for junior and senior high. (*Boarding*. It turned out to be a terrible word. Flat and hard and full of splinters.)

Christina had never been in a school with classrooms, a cafeteria, hallways, bells that rang, art, music, gym, and hundreds of kids. How thrilled she had been when at last, like Anya Rothrock, and Michael and Benjamin Jaye, she was old enough to get on Frankie's boat with her trunks and bags, and land at the town dock.

This was to be the year of being normal.

The year of being just like everybody else.

She had trembled with the joy of being ordinary.

It was Anya's senior year; Benjamin was a sophomore and Michael a ninth-grader. They would have friends; she would have friends; Michael would be on all the teams; Anya would gleam like a new moon; and Christina would be special and spoiled.

But Anya — lovely Anya, with her black hair like a storm cloud around her fragile, white face — had lost her grip on reality. Anya had been terrified of the sea, of the tides that rose every twelve hours and smashed against the cliffs below the mansion. Anya had been terrified of a poster of the sea that hung on her wall and seemed to change texture and color with Anya's sanity.

Slowly Christina had seen the truth. Perched on the cliff over the glittering sea, with its cupola and many roofs — Schooner Inne looked romantic on the outside. But inside . . . the Shevvingtons were destroying Anya on purpose and enjoying every minute of it.

No parent saw it. No matter what Christina explained to Michael and Benj — who were right there, who should have seen! — they just got irritated. "Stop telling yarns, Chrissie," they would say. And sometimes they even complained to the Shevvingtons, "Christina's yarning again." The Shevvingtons convinced Michael and Benj that Christina made up these things in order to attract attention.

The only teacher who realized what was happening, Christina's math teacher, was fired.

So Christina turned to Blake, Anya's boyfriend. Handsome, preppy Blake, who dressed in catalog Maine clothing, and whose watches cost more than a lobster boat. Anya and Blake had walked and danced and kissed, looking like a photograph in a slick magazine. They could have been modeling jeans or perfume or fast cars.

But even with Blake there, Anya collapsed. Her honor grades vanished like snow in the sun; her mind faltered; she quit high school. Blake struggled on; Blake never gave up.

But there was nothing the Shevvingtons did not plan for.

Somehow they arranged for the creature in the wet suit to entice Blake into chasing him. Their timing was perfect. As the twenty-foot tide rolled in like a living army, cannonading off the cruel cliffs,

Blake was to be dashed to pieces. But even the Shevvingtons could not plan for the lucky chance of a tourist strolling by. Blake was saved, though he was in the hospital for weeks. But he went straight from the hospital to the boarding school, and for Anya it was the final blow. She never saw Blake again; Mr. and Mrs. Lathem, his parents, refused even to give Anya Blake's address and phone number, because they held Anya responsible for everything that happened to Blake.

Oh, Blake had phoned once or twice. But he was swept up in another world now, and who knew what he believed about what the Shevvingtons and his parents had told him? And so they had lost Blake, their only ally.

But Christina, golden hair bright as summer apples, silver hair bright as stars, fought back. She was of the island: she was granite, like the rock she was born on, and nothing would stop Christina.

She had shown the Shevvingtons a thing or two! They finally saw she could keep Anya from falling off both the real cliff of the sea and the mental cliff of her mind.

There had been a week — a wonderful moon-bright week — in which Christina knew herself, age thirteen, to be stronger than the principal. The Shevvingtons had bowed down to Christina.

And then, laughing in the way of adults, who are always more powerful in the end, the Shevvingtons had brought forth Dolly, Michael and Benjamin Jaye's little sister. Christina's best friend on the island. Dolly was supposed to be in sixth grade, safe on the island for another whole year. But Mr. Shevvington used his power as principal, announcing that Dolly was "far too bright to be isolated on that remote little island with its pitiful excuse for a school." And Dolly's parents had agreed to let her go to the mainland early.

Had Michael and Benj protested? Had they said "No, no, the Shevvingtons are evil"?

Of course not.

Michael and Benjamin Jaye were oblivious to any of it.

Christmas vacation arrived. The five children went back to the island for two glorious weeks. And on those beautiful December days, filled with sweet song and crispy cookies, never had Burning Fog Isle seemed so remote from the mainland. It was a world of mothers and fathers, of being tucked in at night. It was a world of peace and laughter and people you had known all your life.

Her parents had said gently, "Chrissie, honey, you're exaggerating. You're getting such wonderful grades in school. Writing such fine papers. You seem to have so many friends to write us about, so many interesting activities. It is a terrible shame about Anya, but she's always been fragile, you know."

"The Shevvingtons," Christina said, in her last attempt to convince her parents, "took Anya's fragility and snapped her like little bones."

But they all sighed and said Chrissie was yarning. It was comforting to believe that Michael and

Benj saw nothing because there was nothing to see. Christina even made a New Year's resolution to stop yarning about the Shevvingtons.

They had gone back to Schooner Inne: Michael to basketball, Benj to slog on in school until he turned sixteen and could quit and be a lobsterman; Dolly to sixth grade; Anya to her laundromat; and Christina to her new resolution.

January classes began.

It seemed to Christina in those first days of January that the Shevvingtons hovered over Dolly like birds of prey, circling in the invisible air currents of the threatening sky, waiting for the time to strike. The Shevvingtons were drilling into Dolly's soul with diamond-tipped bits. Christina had no evidence. She hadn't even figured out yet how they were doing it.

She did not know that she had fallen asleep against the cellar door.

The door opened.

Christina fell backward into the kitchen.

The cold, harsh ceiling light blinded her. Blinking, she stared up to see Michael, Benjamin, Dolly, and Mr. and Mrs. Shevvington staring down at her. The Jayes wore jeans. The boys' huge feet were encased in huge, dirty high-top sneakers. Dolly wore tiny, brand-new white sneakers. Mrs. Shevvington's nylons gleamed like water. Mr. Shevvington's creased pant leg rested on his polished leather shoe.

"May I ask, Christina," Mrs. Shevvington said, "why you have chosen to spend your morning in the basement?"

"I was trapped down there," Christina said. She sat up. Now she was staring into their kneecaps. Awkwardly she turned herself over and struggled to her feet. Dolly was giggling. Michael and Benj were shaking their heads in tolerant amusement. "There was somebody down there!" she said. "Somebody — he kept giggling at me."

The boys rolled their eyes. "Chrissie," said Benj, "stop yarning. We've told you and told you. You'll never make friends when you spend all your time yarning."

"It's true," she said. She sounded like a bleating sheep. "Somebody lives in that basement! He's huge and rubbery, and he — "

"What have you been reading!" exclaimed Dolly, giving Christina a little punch in the side. "Chrissie, get a grip on yourself. You're falling apart like Anya."

Anya appeared. She had a tray in her hands. A teacup and a small plate with toast crusts lay on the tray.

"Anya, where were you?" Christina sobbed. "I called and called! You didn't rescue me."

The rest burst into laughter at the idea that Anya could rescue anybody. Anya, frightened by the guffaws, flushed and nearly dropped her tray. Benj rescued the teacup and set the tray down for her. "I was so cold down here," Anya whispered. "And you went away, Chrissie. I went up to my room.

It's safer up there, so high. Away from the waves. Things don't reach me there."

Mr. Shevvington lost his temper. "Christina, look what you've done. Anya was improving. Now you've terrified her again. She's lost all the ground she gained. Why do you do these rotten things, Christina? I think you purposely plan to destroy poor Anya's self-esteem." He turned to Anya. "Christina loves to exaggerate, Anya, dear. You must learn to ignore everything she says."

Dolly giggled softly.

Christina hardened her jaw to keep from showing hurt.

Mrs. Shevvington said, "Wipe that expression off your face, young lady. March back into that cellar."

Christina backed up against Michael and Benj. Save me! she thought. Don't make me go back down there ever again!

The boys pushed her to Mrs. Shevvington, who said, "I will escort you, Christina. We will examine every room. We will look in the dust beneath the furnace, and we will measure the spaces behind the unused sawhorses. Then you will march back up here and admit to everybody that this is yet another of your attempts to get attention."

Chapter 3

"Aw, Christina," said Jonah. He was laughing at her! Christina grew hot with hurt and anger. How could her best friend — a boy who was always saying he wanted to be *better* friends, be a real *boyfriend* — not believe her story? "You have the most active imagination in the state of Maine," he teased. "You see a fishing boat out at sea and you think it's an invading navy. One seal pops its head up in the harbor and you're sure that little brown thing means the harbor is mined with bombs."

Christina stalked away. How could she ever have found Jonah pleasant company? How could she ever have thought he would understand anything?

Jonah ran to catch up. "It was probably just Anya up in the kitchen, being crazy," Jonah offered. "Giggling to herself." Jonah was growing at such a great rate that his blue jeans, new in November, were too short for him in January. Even his hair grew more quickly, and it was bunched up in his collar. His huge feet thumped in the school hallway. He didn't have much control over them. He was always running into something. Beside Jonah Christina always felt graceful. It was a nice feeling, and sometimes she was quite grateful to Jonah for being clunky.

But not today.

"Don't be mad, Chrissie," Jonah said.

She wanted to sock him.

"It was dark down there, and you were scared. You're just being silly, is all."

Christina socked him.

Jonah knew her pretty well. He stepped out of range. Holding up his palms like a warrior's shields, he said, "The Shevvingtons are rotten, I agree with that much. But nobody is living in the cellar, Christina."

She stared at those hands. A man's hands on a boy. The feet and the hands were finished growing; the legs and arms were rushing to catch up.

Slowly, as if unsure that his arm would obey his brain's order, Jonah extended his arm and put it around her shoulder.

What comfort! The weight and the warmth were like a signed contract: *I'm your friend.*

On the island there had been few boys: Dolly's brothers, a couple of little kids in first and second grade, one or two older boys already lobstering for a living. Here in school there were hundreds.

Christina's mind filled and swirled with boys, like a plastic paperweight you shook in your hand to make it snow. In her paperweight were all the seventh-grade boys and of course Blake . . . but in her heart they vanished, as if covered by snow. There was only Jonah. Her eyes and ears filled up with him. She forgot school, its hum of talk, the beginning of classes.

"We'll be late for English," Jonah whispered, as if it were a secret. They took each other's hands, and his hand was very hot in hers. It was like holding a fever.

Mrs. Shevvington stood in front of the blackboard. She held a sheaf of corrected papers in her hand. In her class the seventh-graders, even the boys, were subdued. Nobody had a set of dueling pistols that shot heavy-duty rubber bands into the girls' rear ends. Nobody had forged love letters to pass around the room.

Yet again Mrs. Shevvington made them write an essay in class. Her voice cut like the wind at ten below zero. "A brief essay," she said to her silent thirteen-year-olds, "on January daydreams. One or two paragraphs. Good adjectives. Nothing dull. What you daydream about on the longest, darkest days of winter."

They wrote. The usual kids tried to get sent to the nurse, and Mrs. Shevvington as usual replied that they were welcome to throw up in the wastebasket if necessary, but she expected a finished essay first. The timer on her deck ticked mercilessly. Christina scribbled. She broke her pencil point, and Jonah silently handed her a new pencil. I love you, she thought, but he had looked back at his own paper before their eyes met.

"Time," said Mrs. Shevvington triumphantly. As always, Gretchen and Vicki collected the essays, their mean little faces smirking down on the pages, knowing trouble was out there for somebody — but not them. Never them. Mrs. Shevvington leafed slowly through the sheaf of essays. Nobody breathed. They were all praying not to be ordered to read theirs aloud. Mrs. Shevvington tapped the papers rhythmically against her palm, as if spanking herself.

"Christina?" said Mrs. Shevvington. "Read, please. We will all be so interested in what you have to say."

The class sagged in relief. Christina could handle anything. It was better for her to be Mrs. Shevvington's victim than any of them.

Gretch and Vicki stroked their silken hair in identical motions and leaned back in their chairs, the better to laugh at Christina.

Christina walked to the front of the class. She knew her essay was good, even funny. So why was she picked? What torment awaited her? Mrs. Shevvington handed her the paper. For once there was an expression on the teacher's flat face, but Christina could not fathom it. It was power, that much she knew. Whatever was going to happen, Mrs. Shevvington had planned it.

The panic from the cellar rose up in Christina. All things dark and slimy trembled in her brain. She tried to control her voice, but couldn't. It quivered. Even her chin shook. In her hand the essay trembled.

Gretch exploded in a silvery giggle.

Christina looked at Jonah for support. His smile

gave her courage. She began reading out loud. " 'My January Dream. By Christina Romney. I have cabin fever. The snow, the cold, the ice, and the early dark are like demons. I am going winter mad. The sweater I put on so eagerly when the first cold wind came up in September had the prettiest pattern. It was cozy on my shoulders. Now the same sweater is an instrument of torture. My January dream is of burning all my winter clothes. I have worn the same heavy sweaters and the same thick flannel shirts week after week after week. In my January dream I light a huge bonfire in the middle of a field of snow. We all throw our old boring winter clothes into the fire. Then we feel a thousand times better, and we can laugh all the way through February.' "

Christina finished. How clever the essay sounded. Surely the others felt the same way about their winter wardrobes. She half thought her classmates would applaud, and she got ready to smile back.

But instead, Vicki screamed with laughter. "Then you'd be naked all through February, Christina."

Gretchen said pityingly, "The rest of us have tons of clothes. Why, I've hardly even started to show off my sweater collection. I have thirty-four sweaters. How many do you have, Christina?"

Vicki said to Mrs. Shevvington, "Maybe we could get up a collection for Christina. So she'd have something decent to wear."

Mrs. Shevvington said that island girls had too much pride to accept charity, but it was very, very thoughtful of Vicki to think of such a thing. Fine people like Vicki, she told the class, were always putting others first.

Christina found her way to her seat. She could feel Jonah's pity. She hated pity. She didn't love him anymore, if that's what that minute of heat and touch had been.

Vicki touched Christina's sweater sleeve and said, "It really is ratty, Chrissie. Maybe you should just wash your wardrobe once this winter and that would make you feel better." Vicki and Gretch laughed together, like music boxes, all tinkly. Christina yearned to throw the silver laughter against the wall and smash it.

Mrs. Shevvington delivered a strange little lecture as she walked up and down the rows of desks. "January daydreams," she repeated. "Daydreams are dangerous things, children. You must be very sure you want what you daydream of." She was right in front of Christina's desk, and her heavy-lidded eyes in the oatmeal of her face stared at Christina. "Sometimes when things come true," said Mrs. Shevvington softly, her voice crawling into Christina's ears like mice in the night, "you are sorry."

Class, like all tortures, ended eventually.

The rest of school was a summer breeze compared to English. At lunch Christina looked for Jonah. Ahead of her in the hall she saw Mr. Shevvington. In his hand he held a large, swollen briefcase. Christina had never seen it before. It was old but cherished. The leather was supple, kept soft and shiny with polish.

He loves that briefcase, Christina thought.

She stood quietly among the teenagers going to and from the most important thirty minutes of the day — lunch. Mr. Shevvington entered his office. A few minutes later he came out again — without the briefcase.

Christina slipped into the girls' bathroom to avoid notice.

While she was there a thought crossed her mind.

She took a paper towel from the shiny box on the wall. She folded it several times. She waited while girls entered and left the stalls, brushed their hair, played with lip gloss. When she was alone Christina unlocked a window, opened it a quarter inch, and wedged the paper in the crack so that the window would not lock.

Chapter 4

After school Christina stood near the playing fields waiting for Dolly.

The wintry days were so short! Class was hardly over when the sky began getting dark. January closed in like a fat dictionary on a pressed flower. Christina felt squashed between the pages of January days.

She swung her ice skates in a circle.

The village fire department had ruled that nobody could skate on the pond this year. It never froze hard enough because of the brook flowing beneath it. Instead, the parking lot behind the old hardware store was flooded. The curbs held a few inches of water, which froze smooth and black, and there the children skated safely.

Christina was just an ordinary skater, but when she laced up her skates, she felt like an Olympic star, and in her head she heard nations applauding.

Dolly came running down the street from elementary school, her book bag, skates, and scarf flying behind her like separate people.

You could never mistake Dolly for anyone else. Her thick red hair was still in two braids, because she was only in sixth grade and had not started to care yet about hair. Her skinny little legs and long thin arms flung about her as if they were barely stapled to her body and might come off if you jerked too hard. Dolly never cared if any of her clothing matched. Today she wore a neon-pink ski jacket and killer-whale-blue pants with a screaming yellow scarf.

Dolly always had so much to say; she began talking long before she was close enough to be heard, so Christina came into the middle of Dolly's conversation. " . . . because of people watching. I fall down too much. I'd rather read about skating than actually skate. So we won't go to the parking lot ice. People would laugh at me. We'll go to the pond." She took Christina's hand. Dolly was a great hand-holder. She held hands with teachers and boys, crossing guards, and cafeteria aides.

"We can't skate on the pond," objected Christina. "There are rules now."

"I hate rules," Dolly said. Dolly believed the entire world should revolve around her, and it often did. Dolly had been born on Thanksgiving Day and her mother let them use Dolly for Baby Jesus in that year's Christmas pageant. She was only four weeks old and a ten-year-old Mary had dropped Dolly headfirst into the manger. There wasn't any brain damage, the doctor who had flown in told them. (Her older brothers always said there was plenty.) Dolly wanted to be Baby Jesus every year. She thought it was boring to have Jesus always either in diapers or dying on a cross, and they should have a nice six-year-old Jesus (Dolly) or a really decent nine-year-old Jesus (Dolly).

Nobody could pout quite as well as Dolly if things did not go her way.

But everything was going her way right now. While Christina felt farther away from Burning Fog Isle than Siberia, Dolly had not been homesick once. Christina could get so homesick she'd open a window and let the wind carry her tears back to the island, but Dolly simply adopted the Shevvingtons as parents. And no matter how many warnings Christina issued, Dolly never listened.

Dolly said, "You don't really want to skate, do you? Let's go home and be cozy and read." Dolly's life was stacked with books. Books to underline, to read under the covers, to read out loud to Christina.

Christina could not imagine wasting a daylight hour on the written word. "Please, Dolly? I love to skate." Christina wrapped her scarf around her throat. She loved the soft woolen caress under her chin. "Look at that field. Untouched snow!" cried Christina. "Let's make a chain of angels."

They lay down in the snow, swinging their legs and arms outward to make robes and wings, then stepping carefully across the fresh snow to make the next angel. Christina yearned for some of the toughest seventh-grade boys, so she could have a snowball fight. Christina believed in serious fights.

"I'm too thin for this," Dolly said. "I don't get enough blood to my extremities. I'll die of exposure and it'll be your fault."

"No," Christina said. "Playing in the snow makes you stronger. It's reading all those books that weakens you."

They made an angel chain all the way to the snow fence. "Come on," Christina said. "Let's go to the parking lot after all. They won't laugh at you. I'll hold your hand. We'll skate partners. Then you won't fall."

Dolly shook her head. Christina felt that Dolly was just not interested in her anymore. They were no longer friends, just two people with a history, who were now living in the same building. The Shevvingtons had eaten their way into Dolly's heart like witches through a gingerbread house. Dolly gave them her art projects and dedicated her social studies papers to them.

If the Shevvingtons keep eating at her, Christina thought, Dolly will have no heart left. She will be empty.

The winter shadows were long and blue. The sky drowned the snow in darkness. Emptiness was everywhere: her lungs, the fields, the wide sky. Today it begins again, Christina Romney thought. I can feel it coming. The Shevvingtons are ready to attack.

"Look at the pond," Dolly said, pointing. "It's waist deep in snow. The fire department is just too mean and lazy to clear it." Dolly pouted.

Christina took Dolly's hand again, relieved. Now

they'd have to skate on the parking lot. "You didn't want to skate anyway."

From the pond came a deep groan. Like a grizzly bear. A huge grinding roar like a chewing monster.

The girls stood still as statues in Stone Tag. Their bright jackets were targets in the white snow.

The groan came again. As deep as a cave.

Or a cellar.

"Something's under the ice," Dolly whispered. "It's going to get us!"

The third groan was stronger, as if the ice were attacking.

The girls turned and ran. Across the fields, past the trees. Dolly's braids flew in Christina's face like soft branches. Her yellow scarf flew off, and Christina caught it like an escaped canary. Through the deep snow they staggered. Over the snow fence, up to their chain of angels.

The wind — or something else — had been at work.

None of the angels had heads.

Chapter 5

Puffs of color against the white snow, they ran until they reached the school. But school was long over, and the door was locked.

It amused Christina in a grim way that she was seeking refuge in the building where the Shevvingtons reigned. All the parents admired Mr. Shevvington. When Mr. Shevvington spoke the parents would repeat what he said, as if quoting the President or the *New York Times*.

Dolly and Christina ran around the school, trying two more doors. Locked. "Let's go home," whimpered Dolly.

Home? Christina thought. She was snow-blind in the glare of the setting sun, and she kept seeing those horrible headless angels. There is no home for us, she thought. Home is on an island, far away. All we have are the Shevvingtons and the cellar, where a thing of rubber lives.

"Chrissie, I wanna go home," Dolly said, almost in baby talk.

But Christina had stopped running.

In front of her was an enormous passenger van, sparkling like jewelry. Gretchen's mother drove. Inside, laughing seventh-grade girls and boys were packed.

Christina forgot the pond, the angels, and the groans.

"They're all in your class," Dolly said. "Chrissie, are they going someplace? Why aren't you going, too?"

Gretchen, who practically ran the seventh grade, looked down on Christina. Vicki, beautiful in a black-and-silver ski jacket, smirked from another window.

"I wasn't invited," Christina said.

Was there a more terrible sentence in the world? Her heart ached. Even her joints ached, as if being left out had given her back pain.

All her friends were in the van. They were going to Pizza Power, where they would play video games and eat pizza wedges till they dropped. They saw Christina and waved. You weren't invited. Gretchen and Vicki smacked upright palms, like winners in a tournament. You weren't invited.

The fight went out of Christina. When Dolly still refused to skate at the parking lot, she shrugged. They walked back to Schooner Inne, through the village so loved by tourists, and across the Singing Bridge. From here they could see beyond the harbor and out into the ocean. Their beloved Burning Fog Isle was beyond the horizon.

The wind was so icy it must have come straight from the Arctic. Christina could smell snow in the sky.

Dolly said dreamily, "I have the best library books for tonight. I can hardly wait to start reading." Dolly had the right constitution for reading. When she was tired, she was very tired and would curl up in the old chair and sit for hours, flicking pages. "Sometimes I think it's wrong to spend so much time choosing books," Dolly confided, showing Christina the titles of her weekend choices. "It's probably like a drug. I'll get so addicted to the library shelves I'll cling, sobbing, to the library door when they try to close for the night."

Above them loomed the white bulk of Schooner Inne, its shutters dark and creaking. The front door opened, as if by remote control. Mr. or Mrs. Shevvington must have opened it, but nobody was visible. Only darkness, as if the house had no inhabitants who needed to see. Headless angels, perhaps.

Christina shivered.

But Dolly shouted joyfully, "Hi, Mrs. Shevvington! How are you? Did you have a nice day? Wait till I tell you about my day!" She ran ahead of Christina, swinging her precious books, throwing herself into an invisible embrace.

Wind knocked the doors shut again before Christina got there. She stood alone on the narrow top step, fumbling at the handle.

Tiny flecks of snow, hard as diamonds, whipped her cheeks.

* * *

They had a classic blizzard supper: pancakes, maple syrup, and sausages.

Dolly's two brothers ate like starved animals, pouring maple syrup over melting heaps of butter on top of pancake mountains. Michael, who was a ninth-grader, was on Junior Varsity; he talked about basketball practice, games past, and games to come. Benj, who was a sophomore, worked afternoons at a garage. He talked about transmissions, brake fluid, and fan belts.

Christina thought it remarkable that they cared about these things.

There had been a time when she had been in love with Michael, when she had never been off-island and had no comparison. Now she found Michael self-centered: aware of nothing but teammates and games.

Besides, she had other boys to think of now . . . Jonah, also in seventh grade . . . and Blake.

Blake had been gone for so long. It was difficult to remember Blake the person, but she could imagine him as a photograph: glossy and perfect, his clothes as rich as summer people, his smile as deep as the sea. She had touched his shoulder once, and he had touched hers. Daily Christina had had to remind herself, You're just a little kid. He hardly notices you. He's in love with Anya.

When Blake went away, Christina's memory built him stronger and more brilliant. She thought of him as a demigod, or a Greek hero, who, if only he would return, could save them all.

No other boy measured up to Blake. Benj and Michael were just two more Schooner Inne boarders who were noisier, messier, and hungrier than she was.

Mr. Shevvington sat at one end of the table. His suit today was herringbone gray with an elegant wine-red vest.

Mrs. Shevvington sat at the opposite end of the table. She was opposite her husband in all ways. Thick, graceless, and ugly, her fingers were stubs, like burned-up candles. Whenever she passed a plate, Christina was surprised that those short, fat fingers could even grip the edge.

Poor Anya floated around the table, not coming to rest, not touching the food set out for her. Nobody noticed Anya anymore. She was just a fixture, like a coffee pot or a blender. The lovely dark hair that had once drifted like a cloud around her ivory princess's face was lank and thin. The dark, mysterious eyes were dulled, as if nobody lived behind them anymore; the house of Anya lay empty.

Christina dusted her pancakes with confectioners' sugar instead of maple syrup. She spooned it out of the box and into a tiny sifter, shaking the sifter so that the sugar fell like snow on her food. She didn't like the edges of pancakes any more than she liked the crusts of sandwiches. She cut each bite into a triangle, leaving discarded pancake curves all over her plate.

"Christina," said Mrs. Shevvington, "you are too old to play with your food. Simply eat, please."

She had fought them over food issues before.

They always won. Once when Christina had disobeyed right up to midnight, they had telephoned her parents on the island, and her parents had sided with the Shevvingtons. ("Christina!" said her mother furiously. "What is the matter with you? Going to war over creamed potatoes! Grow up.")

Christina studied her pancake edges. Then she squashed them down with the back of her fork and crammed them all in her mouth at one time. It was like eating wet pillows.

Dolly said, "The sixth grade is getting French Exposure this week."

"What's that?" said her brothers. "Like getting exposed to the sun?"

"We get Spanish Exposure, too," Dolly said. "To see which language we want to take next year in seventh grade, when we study a language for real. I am sure that the French teacher swears when he mutters under his breath. I am memorizing all his swears. Wouldn't it be nice to swear in lots of languages?" Dolly's laugh was like finger cymbals: tiny and tinkling.

Her brothers roared. Their laughter was like lions in a cave. Benj and Michael demanded to be taught the swears.

Outside, the snow came down thick as winter blankets.

Dolly, who had hardly touched her supper, said, "Ooooooh, that was good, Mrs. Shevvington." She slipped out of her chair, slowly circled the big ugly table with its legs as thick as thighs, and rested her head on Mrs. Shevvington's shoulder. Mrs. Shevvington did not yell at her for not finishing her milk and eating only the middles of the pancakes.

Dolly drew her two braids around her mouth, like a Christmas wreath. "You know what?" she said through her hair. "Christina made me go skating. We went to the pond, and — "

"What!" cried Mr. Shevvington. He swung his distinguished face in Christina's direction. The eyes were blue today and as cold as the tips of Dolly's fingers. "Christina Romney! I am appalled. You took Dolly to that unsafe ice?"

His eyes today were bright blue, like a husky dog ready to bite. Mr. Shevvington's stare slowed her brain. Christina's tongue stumbled, trying to explain.

Dolly's brothers remembered there were things in life besides basketball and cars. "Christina!" Benjamin yelled at her. "You're the one who's older! You're supposed to take care of Dolly!" His big bony face, shadowed where he was starting a beard, was dark with anger.

"What's the matter with you, you jerk?" Michael said.

Christina waited for Dolly to admit that it had been *her* idea.

But Dolly said nothing. She snuggled closer to Mrs. Shevvington and Mrs. Shevvington rocked her like a baby.

Mr. Shevvington's eyes glittered at Christina like beach pebbles. "The pond, indeed! Do you want Dolly to fall through the ice and drown?" Mrs. Shevvington pointed her fat index finger at Christina.

The nail was bitten down into the quick, but she had polished it anyway, red as blood.

"Dolly, tell them what happened," Christina ordered.

Dolly said, "We made angels in the snow. The wind blew their heads away. Like executions. And then the ice on the pond screamed at us."

"Expansion," said her brother Benj. "When ice gets colder or warmer it expands and contracts. Makes terrible noises."

Mrs. Shevvington smiled, exposing her horrid little teeth, yellow as birdseed. She played with Dolly's thick braids. "Dolly, darling, what are you going to do tonight?"

They were finished with Christina. The Shevvingtons would pay no more attention to her that night.

Anya drifted, thin as paper, having said nothing, perhaps having thought nothing, certainly having eaten nothing.

I just became a tiny bit like Anya, Christina thought. Empty. Invisible. Why, Dolly can't be bothered to stick up for me. Even to Michael and Benj, I am nobody. That's how the Shevvingtons destroy. Look what they did to Val, Robbie's sister! Robbie doesn't even call her by name. Now it's happening to me. Even to my own mother and father, I'm just a person who ought to obey the Shevvingtons.

"Read," said Dolly with immense satisfaction. "I have two mysteries, two romances, and two science fiction."

Mr. Shevvington said, "You are reading too much, Dolly, my dear. A well-rounded young lady uses her body as well as her mind. You must become an athlete."

Dolly shuddered. "I'd rather read about sports. How about if I get out a really great book about ballet? Or horses?"

Her brothers lost interest. They attacked dessert.

"I may just have to suspend your library privileges," Mr. Shevvington teased.

"I'm going to read in bed," Dolly said, ignoring all suggestions of athletic activity. She hoisted her stack of books slowly, as if eating supper had exhausted her. "I've always thought I would make an excellent invalid," she told the Shevvingtons. "I like bed. I like sheets and pillows. I'd lie there and read. All I need is enough strength to turn the pages."

"Perhaps you could have an accident," said Mrs. Shevvington softly.

Christina's blood seemed to stop flowing. Would the Shevvingtons really go that far?

"I would be very brave," Dolly agreed.

Down the length of the kitchen table, the Shevvingtons smiled at each other.

Chapter 6

When Schooner Inne lay silent in the night, when the snow had stopped and the tide was out, Christina left her bedroom. She crept in the dark around the tilting balcony with its little forest of white railings. Down the bare, slippery stair she tiptoed, hand sliding on the old bent rail.

Hardly breathing, she paused on the second floor, where the pretty guest rooms and the Shevvingtons' beautiful master bedroom surrounded the lower balcony. There was no sound.

The mansion and its inhabitants slept.

The next set of stairs was carpeted: rich, soft, toe-tickling carpet.

At the bottom, Christina knelt and put on her boots and jacket. She checked her house keys, zipped them carefully into her side pocket, and slid out of Schooner Inne.

The night sky was so clear Christina felt she could taste the stars. If she opened her lips and stuck out her tongue, the stars would fall like snowflakes and taste like bitter lemons.

It was two o'clock in the morning. The village was silent. No cars stirred. No lights were on in houses. Nothing moved but a small thirteen-year-old girl named Christina Romney.

She walked one block and turned a corner. Her shadow leapt ahead, like a black giant. The only sound was the light crunch of her own boots in the snow.

Behind her the snow crunched.

Christina's heart crunched with it. She spun on the street, whirling to face the crunch. From the cellar? she thought numbly. No, no, it couldn't have heard me.

Headlights wheeled around the corner. The faint roof light of a police car twinkled.

Christina backed into the doorway of the nearest shop.

A police car was not reassuring when you were planning to break into a building.

But the police had not seen her. The men in the car looked straight ahead, cruising by in boredom. When they had vanished, Christina crept on in the dark toward her school.

In the night the school loomed like a monster with square edges: dark and wicked in the moon-tinted snow. She pulled off her ski cap, letting her tri-colored hair fall free. Nobody had hair like Christina. She counted on her silver and gold locks to protect her from the demons of the dark.

The winter wind bit through Christina's heavy coat. Who would have thought she would start the second semester with breaking and entering?

What if I get caught? Christina thought, flattening herself against an icy brick wall. In the blackness she could not see herself. Her shadow no longer existed: she was a non-person.

If I get caught, it will be exactly what the Shevvingtons want. But nobody else can stop the Shevvingtons. "Maybe you could have an accident," they had whispered down the table.

The Shevvingtons had a grip on the adult community like it was a dog on a leash. No parent, no grown-up, no teacher would save Dolly.

She knew the Shevvingtons well. Other people might rent a movie or read a library book for weekend entertainment, but the Shevvingtons loved to gloat. Somewhere, someplace lay a stack of papers and photographs of all their previous victims.

Last fall she had believed any incriminating papers would be in the Guidance Office. There had been no papers there, though, only computer disks, and she had gotten caught trying to find the right disk.

Then she had searched every inch of Schooner Inne. She had even looked and measured for secret compartments and hidden backs on cabinets and bookcases.

But there was nothing at Schooner Inne except the weird whistle of the wind off the Atlantic Ocean crying, "Ffffffffffff!" until Christina grew dizzy and sick trying not to hear it.

But now she knew about the briefcase. A container Mr. Shevvington stroked like a pet.

Christina could imagine Mr. Shevvington . . . the

office door locked . . . his secretary told to hold telephone calls . . . she could see his fine suit, his gleaming vest, the dashing little scarf he liked to wear . . . taking a beloved file from the deep, dark leather. How well she knew that private, gloating smile.

The power of adults! How they could humiliate a child in class. How easily they could manipulate and frighten. How they could control a child's future by vicious rumor or carefully planned coincidence.

Anya had been the hope and pride of Burning Fog Isle. And now, thanks to hard work on the Shevvingtons' part, Anya was a high school dropout who worked at the laundromat, folding other people's clothing . . . if she remembered how. And the Shevvingtons were so clever! They convinced everybody that it was Anya's fault. "Poor Anya has a week character," they said.

Before Anya, the victim had been Robbie's sister Val. Christina would always remember Robbie's warning, when school started last fall. "You're new here, Christina. You've been out on that island, protected from things. You don't know. Be careful of the Shevvingtons."

And Christina had said, "Why?"

"I had an older sister," he replied, giving the sister no name, no description, as if she were truly not a person, just a thing. Robbie's eyes were sad and dark.

But later Christina found out. Her name was Val. She was even worse than Anya. She'd been stuck in an institution. Was still there. "Why don't your parents do something about the Shevvingtons?" Christina had cried.

Robbie raised his eyebrows. "They are grateful to the Shevvingtons," he said quietly. "For trying so hard to help Val. For finding her a counselor, and when that didn't work, for helping them put Val away."

So among the files Mr. Shevvington would smile over would be Val's. He had truly triumphed with Val. There was nothing at all left of her.

Before Val, Christina had no knowledge. The Shevvingtons had not been in Maine before that.

I will find out, Christina thought. I will get the truth. I will stop the Shevvingtons before they can fill any folders full of Dolly or me.

A pink overhead light in the parking lot buzzed like a swarm of hornets. Christina gripped a wire trash basket and rolled it over the ice-pocked snow. She stood it up under the girls' bathroom window.

What if Mr. Shevvington had gone into the bathroom to check, once he'd spotted her coming out? What if he knew her errand? What if he had heard her sneaking out of Schooner Inne and gotten here ahead of her?

The rhythm of her breathing was frantic. Her lungs slammed against her ribs. She climbed on top of the garbage can. With cold fingers she felt the window sill.

Neither the janitors nor Mr. Shevvington had found her folded paper towel. She forced her fingers under the crack and opened the window.

Swinging one foot in, Christina rested her stomach on the sill and then lowered herself sideways inside the school. Her heart was pounding so hard her chest hurt. She took the flashlight out of her inside jacket pocket and turned it on.

The compartments and sinks of the girls' bathroom glittered cold and metallic. The dozen mirrors threw Christina's reflection back and forth. She crept out of the bathroom. The door shut silently and slowly behind her.

There were no windows in the halls.

The darkness was complete. As sick, as abnormal as the Shevvingtons.

The thin circle of light from her flash was pitiful. Her hand shook with fear, and the light shivered with her wrist.

Somebody in the blackness was breathing.

Christina froze like an icicle. She could not think.

The breathing was heavy and irregular and thick. It — it —

— it's me, she thought. I'm so scared I'm panting.

She leaned against the wall for a moment, remembering gym exercises. Three deep breaths, she told herself. She sucked air into her lungs, held it, heaved it out. Three times.

It actually worked. She was calmer. She moved her feet again. Left. Right. Left.

She was strong with purpose, as strong as the island granite from which she had come. They can't stop me, Christina thought proudly.

She forgot how many girls they had stopped before her. Girls who were older, stronger, smarter.

Chapter 7

Mr. Shevvington's office door was open.

This surprised Christina so much she was almost afraid to push it after she found the handle would turn. Could he be waiting inside?

No. If Christina had made any noise leaving Schooner Inne, it had been covered by the slapping of ocean waves. If poor Anya had heard Christina creeping, she'd think it was a ghost and tremble beneath her covers. Michael and Benj slept with their radio on and never heard anything but drums. Dolly slept as only a small child can sleep, thickly and completely.

Now Christina pressed against the outer office wall. With the tip of her toe, she pushed the principal's door, like a policeman afraid the bad guy inside would have a gun.

The door moved without sound and without resistance. But it did not stay open. She had to hold it. She was terrified it would close on her, trap her inside Mr. Shevvington's office, like a lobster in a trap: easy to crawl in, impossible to back out.

She used a huge telephone book to prop the door open.

She planned to touch nothing. Mr. Shevvington might even use fingerprints against her. Her mother's hand-knitted mittens would keep her fingers safe.

The briefcase sat by the desk, half in the cavity where his feet went. Where he could reach down, just as Christina had imagined, to stroke its leather skin and remember gladly what it held.

Christina lifted the briefcase. It was full. These have to be the papers I want! she thought.

She did not want to turn on lights to examine the papers. She did not want to be there another second longer than she had to. She would take the brief-case —

But where?

She could not hide it in her bedroom at Schooner Inne. It was too small, too barren, for hiding places. She could not hide it anywhere else in the Inne either. Mrs. Shevvington spent all her spare time polishing, keeping the Inne gleaming for the guests who never came. Perhaps Anya's laundromat — that hot, damp back room full of lint and lost socks?

Christina slipped out of the office, letting the door close. It made a little *snick*. She put the telephone book back exactly as it had been. She let herself out into the hall.

Far down the hall, an EXIT sign gleamed hot pink and dusty.

A man stood under the sign, his shoulders pink with EXIT light. He laughed, a low, insane giggle.

His dark rubbery body gleamed. She knew he was a man by his great size — and yet he was too smooth-edged to be a person. He was something else. Something not human.

Giggling, the thing moved fluidly toward her as if underwater . . . swimming Christina's way.

She felt underwater herself — eyes, brain, lungs, and legs clogged with terror.

The thing waved at Christina.

It swam down the hall, arms out to catch her.

There was nowhere to go but down the hall.

Christina fled toward the opposite EXIT sign. But it was blockaded by a diamond-crossed grill — one of the moveable walls strung out to block the halls at night, so the people who came to the basketball games in the gym could not just cruise throughout the school.

The rubbery, giggling thing had long legs — much longer than Christina's. Nor was the thing weighed down by a heavy briefcase.

It came so close Christina could even smell it. It smelled like low tide — like the ocean in summer.

Christina swerved into the gym.

It was black as velvet in there. She turned off her flashlight and scooted under the bleachers. She ran down into the middle of them and crouched, motionless.

Her lungs refused to stay motionless. They heaved, sucking in air as if they belonged to somebody else entirely. *Sssssshhhh*, she said to her lungs and *Hhhhhhhhh*, her lungs said back, screaming for oxygen.

The gym doors clanked open.

For a horrible moment the gleaming creature was framed in the faint pinkish light from the center hall.

Then the gym door closed.

It was in the gym with Christina.

Getting closer, coming toward her as if he could see in the dark. As if the whites of her eyes or the heaving of her lungs was a sign to him. The giggle was part groan, part insanity.

The scent of the sea was so strong it was like the tide coming in. Did he live underwater? Was he human? Did the Shevvingtons' evil extend to some other world Christina could not even imagine?

The thing approached the bleachers — not from the side, where he could slip in where she hid and grab her — but from the front, where he could push the bleachers together. Shove them against the wall.

Crush Christina.

She was hollowed out with fear. So this was how Anya felt — kneeling, helpless, caught — a victim. Without an exit, without hope.

The creature in the wet suit pushed the first row of bleachers under the second row. She was staring at his knees, and then his knees vanished because he shoved both those rows under the third row. He was making a wood-and-metal wall. He would shove on until there was no room for Christina. *Until there was no Christina.*

The bleachers protested. They clanked. Their joints fought back a little bit.

Christina, of the island, strong as granite, choked back sobs. She would not beg. She would not plead. She would not give in!

She had her proof in her hand, but there would be a different kind of proof in the morning.

The body of Christina Romney.

I want my mother! Christina thought. She clung to the mittens her mother had knit her. They gave her strength. There was love knit into that wool. Duck walking, Christina crept toward the side.

Now the thing pushed the three stacked bleachers under the fourth. He had to use his shoulder to force them, but all it cost him was a little grunt. Usually it took the whole basketball team to shut the bleachers.

He's so strong, she thought.

Christina emerged at her edge.

If he catches me . . . Christina thought.

She waited until he was throwing his shoulder against the stacked seats. Then she ran.

She fled the gym, flinging the door open. She skidded on the waxed linoleum and raced down the hall to the girls' room. Please let me get in here and close the door before he sees where I'm going! she prayed.

In the bathroom she was reflected in the mirrors: fear was painted on her face like a melted, deformed Barbie doll.

She climbed up onto the window sill but couldn't get a grip with her mittens on. She slipped back onto the floor.

Behind her the bathroom door opened and the

giggle pierced the room like knives.

Christina dived face first out the window, missing the trash can by inches, and falling instead onto a mattress of new-fallen snow.

The weather had changed as it did in Maine, instantly and without warning. She leaped to her feet and ran on. In the parking lot horrible buzzing lights illuminated her like a moth to be stabbed on a pin.

She ran across the playing fields toward the village.

Snow blew in her face and obscured her vision.

For three steps she ran on top of the snow. Then her foot broke through the crust. She floundered up to her knees. The wind whistled around her head and through the three colors of her hair as if she were a barn roof.

She could not hear the giggle, but that was because the snow had become a storm, and the Atlantic Ocean was pounding and the wind shrieking. She came to the Singing Bridge, whose open iron fretwork made the car tires hum when they passed over. The iron was solid with ice. With each splash of the extremely high tide, another slick layer was added.

To get to Schooner Inne she had to cross the Singing Bridge.

It will sweep me away, thought Christina Romney. The sea will take me down into Candle Cove and take me out with the tide. I will be frozen solid, like a maiden in an old poem: all ice. Even my heart and soul.

Exactly what the Shevvingtons want.
They planned this.
They knew.
They're inside even now.
Laughing.

Chapter 8

She clung to a steel cable.

The mittens her mother had knit her were double layered: black with white angora stars. The yarn froze to the steel, and the leaping seawater soaked the mittens, freezing them into hand-shaped curls.

I was wrong, thought Christina Romney, her hands frozen to the bridge. It was not Dolly they were after. It was me.

The air from the ocean was so full of salt and snow that she could actually see the wind.

Christina was lashed to the bridge by the very mittens her mother had knitted her. She pulled her hands out of the mittens, leaving them frozen to the steel. "You won't win!" she shouted to the wind. "I am Christina of granite. So there!"

She fought the wind like a wrestler until she got off the Singing Bridge. She turned her back on the wind and half crawled up Breakneck Hill Road. She reached the huge green double doors of Schooner Inne. She found her key in her pocket. Her frozen blue fingers forced it into the lock. She opened the door, slipped in, and shut it behind her. The wallpaper was flocked and formal, put up by the sea captain of so long ago. But the air in the house was chilled, infected by the Shevvingtons.

Christina's throbbing heart did not supply enough energy for the climb to her room. I am old, thought Christina. Perhaps my hair is gray now, instead of silver and gold and chocolate.

She touched her hair, but all she felt was melting snow. I don't have the briefcase. I dropped it somewhere.

She stared at her empty hands. How, oh how could she have done this? Gone through such torture, only to have lost the documents — the proof?

She began crying.

She hung up her coat. She took off her sneakers and set them to dry over the heating vent. She peeled off her soaking socks. The ice that clung to them melted in her hands. She looked up the whirling stairs and the white banisters that blurred like a forest. The first flight was not so bad. Thick plush carpet softened the way for her frozen toes.

The second flight, bare and slippery wood, was cruel and unwelcoming. This is home? Christina Romney thought. This is where I live?

At the top of the stairs, out of the dark behind the balcony came a waft of white. White that swirled like snow or ghosts. Christina was enveloped in white.

She tried to scream, but the white smothered her.

"It's me, Anya," whispered the white. "Where

been, Chrissie? The Shevvingtons came checked your bed, and when they saw you w n't in it, they laughed and went back to their room. Where have you been? Are you all right?"

Anya's swirling lacy nightgown, like a bride's trousseau, folded around Christina. "You're freezing," Anya whispered. "Come, I'll get in bed with you. Body heat will help." They tiptoed to Christina's room. It was tiny and dark, with bare floors and cracked plaster. Christina had added flower pictures and her mother's vivid quilt and a little white rug, but the room stayed dark. There were times when Christina and The Dark were like best friends, huddled together under the covers. But tonight The Dark was laughing, ready to bring out its real friends, creatures of the shadows and the sea.

Anya peeled away Christina's soaking jeans and hung them to dry. The wind came through the electrical outlets in prong-shaped drafts. "I turned on the electric blanket after the Shevvingtons left," Anya whispered, "so the mattress would get hot for you."

Usually Christina hated the electric blanket. She wanted the layers of wool to weight her down. Now the hot blanket was hope and safety.

"There," said Anya, rubbing Christina's feet, "you're all right now." Under the covers, they wrapped their arms around each other until Christina stopped shivering.

"Anya?" said Christina.

"Mmmmm?"

"Are you back?"

"What do you mean, Chrissie? I've never been away. I've lived here for a long, long time."

"But — you waited up for me." Be sane again, Anya, pleaded Christina silently, like prayers. Be my friend, I need a friend, I need you on my side. And you're older than me. Oh, Anya, I want somebody older than me! When I was a little girl on the island, I always wanted to be the oldest. I wanted to be in charge and decide everything and run the show.

I was wrong, Anya. It's awful being the oldest.

Anya, be the oldest! Come back! I need you, Anya.

"I hardly ever sleep," Anya said. "I just lie there and listen to the sea. The sea keeps count, you know. It wants one of us. I don't mind if it's me. But I don't want it to be you."

She still isn't back, Christina thought. I can't tell her about tonight. I still don't have an ally. It isn't the sea who is the enemy.

Christina wanted to weep for Anya or for herself. But she was too tired. She slept.

Anya lay awake, her black hair draping the pillows. She dreamed no dreams; she thought no thoughts. She was empty.

In the morning, at breakfast, Christina clung to Anya. She thought that Mr. Shevvington was watching her more than usual and that Mrs. Shevvington bent closer than usual, but perhaps she was wrong. Mr. Shevvington's soul was hidden by his elegant clothing, and he stayed smooth and gleaming, no matter how dirty his deeds. Mrs. Shevvington's soul was hidden by a body so thick and solid it had no feminine curves whatsoever. Her little black eyes were holes in her flat face, and when she smiled her little yellow teeth lay in rows like corn on the cob.

They did not look as if they belonged together. Grown-ups were always startled when they first met Mr. Shevvington's **wife**, with her complexion like oatmeal. What does he see in her? they would whisper afterwards, for he was inspiring and she was a pudding.

Dolly sat, thin as a rag doll, in her chair next to Mrs. Shevvington. "I washed the windows in my bedroom again," she said, her voice high and trembly.

Salt spray from the whipping waves below the cliffs constantly turned the windows opaque. Christina loved the feathery scrawls of frost, but Dolly whimpered. "They close me up," she said fretfully to Christina. "They stitch me inside my room. They turn my room into the inside of a sleeping bag."

"Don't say that out loud," Christina whispered. "You must not let the Shevvingtons hear you say that."

But Dolly thought Christina was just being hard. She turned to Mr. Shevvington and told him, because he cared when a person was afraid of something. "Poor Dolly," he said. "You're afraid you might suffocate, aren't you?" He smiled.

Then he walked them to the front door, checking that everybody had a book bag and gym shoes.

"And there's another thing," said Dolly, although Christina was signaling her not to talk about it. "I don't like the balcony or the way the bathroom door opens onto the stairs. I don't even like the stairs. Please, may I have a bedroom on the second floor instead? Nobody ever stays in the guest rooms. Please, may I have a guest room? So I don't have to go all the way up to the third floor? I'm afraid I'll fall. At night I can't even go to the bathroom because I'm afraid I might trip over the railing." Dolly shivered with her fear of heights.

"You must learn to cope with your fears," said Mr. Shevvington.

"Why?" said Christina. "Why not just change bedrooms?"

Mr. Shevvington said that Christina did not want anybody but herself to be strong. That Christina approved of Dolly being weak and afraid. "That way you will always have a meek little follower," Mr. Shevvington said.

Christina would have stayed to argue, but Michael and Benj were running down the steps, heading for school. Today of all days, Christina did not want to be alone with a Shevvington. She dragged Dolly after the boys. At the bottom of Breakneck Hill, Dolly turned left for the elementary school. Christina walked in the boys' footsteps through the snow. How would she get through the school days now, knowing what lurked in those halls by night?

Michael and Benj threw snowballs at everything that moved.

Would she see a mound of snow the size of a briefcase?

Or had the giggling creature found it and put it back under the knee cavity of the principal's desk?

In English the essay topic had been "cozy spots." Christina had written about the thickets of blackberry canes on Burning Fog Isle, where she and Michael and Dolly and Benj used to play War. But Mrs. Shevvington chose fat, ugly Katy to read aloud.

" 'I like sitting under the hair dryer at the beauty parlor,' " Katy read. " 'It's a noisy, wheezing, hot-air world. I can't hear anybody's conversations. I read high-fashion magazines and think about being beautiful.' "

Gretch laughed viciously. "At least you can *think* about being beautiful, Katy," she said.

Katy withered and flushed.

Mrs. Shevvington smiled and said nothing. She passed out sets of vocabulary cards. Gretch took advantage of the movement in the room to whisper to Christina, "I'm having a slumber party this Saturday night. You could come this time. I wouldn't mind."

It took all Christina's control not to beat Gretchen black and blue with the vocabulary cards. "I'm afraid I'll be busy," she heard herself say. "I'm having a slumber party of my own."

She could not imagine what had made her say such a thing. The Shevvingtons would never let her have a friend spend the night.

And besides, did she really want the seventh grade to know how the island children lived?

The beautiful parlor downstairs with its black and gold Oriental furniture, furnished by the sea captain from his voyages to China, for his bride. They weren't allowed in there; they might soil something.

The magnificent dining room — nobody could approach that gleaming table; island children might rest their shoes on it.

The adorable guest rooms, with the frilly canopies on the four-poster beds. No, island children were confined to the kitchen, the ugly little back room with the black-and-white television, and their barren rooms on the third floor.

And did she want anybody to see Anya? Seventh-graders were cruel. They would poke fun at Anya, and Anya might be hurt.

Besides, nobody could have fun when Mr. or Mrs. Shevvington was around. It would be the worst slumber party in the history of junior high. Girls would telephone their mothers and ask to be brought home, they would hate it so much.

But all day long, Christina found herself inviting people to the slumber party she could not have.

Jenny was delighted to come. Joanne couldn't wait. Susan and Rebecca and Emily all wanted to come.

Christina found herself madly inviting everybody

she had ever met — everybody whose name she remembered — just so that Gretchen couldn't have them at her party.

What price am I going to pay for this? Christina thought.

Part of her was sick and wanted to run away to California.

The other part of her kept asking more and more girls to come to the party.

Chapter 9

I wish I were beautiful, Christina thought. She twined the silver locks with the gold, and then the gold with the brown. I'm interesting, she thought. I'm unusual. But I'm not beautiful.

She borrowed Anya's hot rollers to set her hair. She thought of poor, fat, ugly Katy, whose favorite cozy nook was the hair dryer at the beautician's.

Suddenly, critically, Anya said, "You have too much hair on each roller. Here. I'll do it for you."

It always surprised Christina when the old Anya surfaced, as if bits and pieces of her were floating around and latched occasionally onto things like hot rollers. Last night she was partly aware, Christina thought. She stayed up for me, warmed my feet. And now tonight she's partly here.

Perhaps the Shevvingtons had misjudged. They thought Anya was completely destroyed, but perhaps she was healing.

The Shevvingtons must not know, Christina thought. They must not see Anya coming back. Or they would go after her again. This time, like Val, they would get her put away.

When Anya gently took Christina's hair off the curlers, gone was the tangle that usually capped her head. Elegant, smooth waves fell past her shoulders and gleamed in the lamplight. She felt older and romantic: she was a woman now, not a mere seventh-grader.

"Me, too!" Dolly cried.

If Dolly sees changes in Anya, thought Christina, she will tell the Shevvingtons.

"Anya, fix my hair," Dolly ordered. Dolly unbraided her hair. The braid pattern stayed in the hair, as if she had been run over by tank treads.

"Leave it like that," suggested Christina.

Dolly looked annoyed. "Make me look older than Christina, Anya," Dolly said.

Anya fussed with Dolly's hair. She arranged it in long, soft loops, like a girl at the turn of the century, and fastened it with hidden bobby pins and one large glittering barrette.

Dolly's prettier than I am, Christina thought. I am granite, like the island. I am strong and tough. But I am not pretty.

For a strange, painful moment she yearned for prettiness more than anything on Earth. It hurt inside, crying out, Let me be pretty, too!

The telephone rang. Mrs. Shevvington answered downstairs, calling up, "It's for you, Christina. Do not stay too long on the phone unless it's homework. The telephone is not a toy. Do not abuse your telephone privileges."

Christina walked sedately down the three flights, because if she ran Mrs. Shevvington would punish her by not letting her take the phone call. "Hello?" she said cautiously. Mrs. Shevvington stood right next to her.

"Hi," said Jonah. He sounded breathless and eager, like somebody going Christmas shopping.

"Hi, Jonah." Her hair was as silver as stars, as golden as summer apples. She felt pretty.

Jonah said, "I had a nice time this afternoon."

She and Jonah had gone skating on the parking lot ice. They had raced, flinging insults and snowballs at each other. It had been loads of fun, but it had not been romantic. A phone call, though, that was romantic.

Mrs. Shevvington's little black eyes were hardly a foot away. "Page ninety-eight," Christina said. "First twenty examples."

Jonah said, "Chrissie. Is this code or is she listening?"

"Both," Chrissie said.

Jonah said, "Let me know what they say about having the slumber party, Chrissie. See if they'll let you have boys come, too. Now that would be fun."

He was flirting with her. She touched her hair, reminding herself she was an elegant woman with gleaming tresses. But Mrs. Shevvington laughed and walked away and Christina turned back into a pumpkin: seventh grade, dumb and young. "See you tomorrow," she said, which was not even conversation, let alone flirting.

It occurred to Christina that there might not be a price to pay for setting up a slumber party. At dinner when she asked for permission, the Shevvingtons would simply say, "Absolutely not. Twenty screaming, animal-like, seventh-grade girls in our perfect inn? Never."

Then at school, Christina would just say, "They wouldn't let me. You'll have to go to Gretch's after all. Too bad."

This began to sound rather nice. It would be the first time this year that Christina had not only gotten herself into trouble, but also out of it.

But to Christina's amazement, the Shevvingtons said, "What a grand idea! Why, Christina, that will be lovely. We'll have such fun! We'll play all kinds of games. We'll make popcorn balls and pull taffy. We'll play hide-and-seek all through the house. We'll draw lots to see which girls get which guest room. You must tell them to bring their very best robes and slippers. We'll have a midnight fashion show and drink hot chocolate before we retire to our suites, like English ladies."

Christina stared at them. They appeared to be serious.

Michael and Benj made faces, groaned, and clutched their throats. Junior-high girls, they announced, were the lowest creatures on earth. They would sleep at friends' houses, so they wouldn't see or help or clean up after this slumber party.

"Who is coming, Christina?" said Mr. Shevvington, his smile still resting on his face, as if he had borrowed it at the library and forgotten to return it.

She rattled off as many names as she could remember, hoping she was not off by more than five or ten.

They made her invite Vicki and Gretchen.

"It's not nice to leave people out," Mr. Shevvington reproved Christina. "If you are going to invite all the others, you really must invite Vicki and Gretchen. Or you will cause hurt feelings." He turned to Mrs. Shevvington. "It's an uphill battle teaching Christina manners, isn't it?"

Mrs. Shevvington nodded sadly.

Michael and Benj did not listen; they had never been interested in good manners. Only sports, food, and cars.

Dolly frowned. "Christina," she said reproachfully. "And you said the Shevvingtons never did anything nice. They're being wonderful to you. Plus, you set up the party before you even asked permission. Chrissie, you owe them an apology."

Christina had planned to warn Dolly yet again: They'd like you to have an accident, Dolly. Then think how they could control you! Every minute and every muscle of you. So be careful. Be careful on stairs, and at the top of Breakneck Hill Road!

But now she was shaking with fury.

"What kinds of games will we play?" Dolly asked, bouncing around.

Christina nearly said, "*You* won't play any of them. I didn't invite *you*. You're only in *sixth*." But she didn't.

Mr. Shevvington stroked the silk scarf he had tied around his throat. He looked like a fashion ad from a Sunday paper. He smiled across the room at no one Christina could see. He said very softly, "A nice game for little girls is Murder. We'll all hide, and I'll choose the victim."

The next day after school Christina stood in the sun waiting for Jonah.

But it was Dolly who found her. Running up, braids swinging — and no books in her arms. Without books, she looked unattached, as if her tiny body might come loose from the earth and blow away in the wind. Christina could hardly remember seeing Dolly without something to read.

Dolly's pixie face puckered with tears. "Mr. Shevvington talked to the elementary school principal about my reading. They agreed that I am too sedentary."

"Too what?"

"I sit too much. They say I have to take dancing lessons. Every single day after school. At Miss Violet's." Dolly's legs and arms flapped like pages of a book. It was hard to imagine her learning graceful patterns for her feet. "I don't want to take dancing. I just want to read, Chrissie. Can't you talk them out of it for me, Chrissie?"

Christina had two fine daydreams. In the first, she ordered the Shevvingtons to let Dolly read books and be sedentary forever and they knelt and obeyed her. In the second, Christina was the dancer — clad in shimmering silver, leaping across the stage to wild applause.

"Walk with me to Miss Violet's?" begged Dolly.

They walked together, Dolly swinging Christina's hand. "Chrissie, what will I do?" Dolly cried. "I'll fall down. I won't be able to learn the steps. I won't get the rhythm right, I'll go in the wrong direction. Everybody will laugh at me."

Miss Violet's School of Dance was a pretty brick building with outside stairs that swooped: the sort of stairs a famous dancer would stand at the top of to receive photographers and journalists who wanted to interview her.

You could fall dancing, Christina thought. Is that what they want Dolly to do? "The Shevvingtons are making you take dancing on purpose," she said. "That's what the Shevvingtons are like."

Mr. Shevvington unfolded like a huge paper doll from a parked car next to Miss Violet's. "Christina," he said sadly. "Still fighting that sick and twisted jealousy, aren't you? We are doing this to help Dolly overcome her fear of failure, to build her frail body and fragile confidence. This is our gift to Dolly. And you, poor girl, are eaten up with jealousy." He patted Christina's shoulder. She wanted to bite him.

Dolly clasped both her hands in front of her, like a child in the nativity scene seeing an angel. "Oh, Mr. Shevvington!" she cried. "*You* paid for the lessons! You are so wonderful! I love you so much!" She turned to Christina. "You don't have to come in with me, Chrissie. Mr. Shevvington's here. I'll be fine now. You go skate in the parking lot. 'Bye."

Jonah and the boys had taken over the parking lot ice. They were speed skating: bent low, thrusting forward, circling as hard and fast as they could. All the little kids had been pushed away and were sitting sadly on the benches over by the tennis courts. All the girls who wanted to practice figure eights or spins had been knocked down enough times that they had given up and left. Christina laced on her skates and skated hard and fast. She pretended her skate blades were slicing Mr. Shevvington.

"Jonah," she said, skating even with him, "do you think I am sick and twisted?"

Jonah grinned. "Sure. That's why I like you. I'm drawn to sick and twisted people."

Jonah's legs were long. It didn't matter how determined Christina was; Jonah could cover more ground. Her muscles cried out for rest, but she disciplined herself, pretending it was the Olympics, her country's honor at stake.

What's really at stake, thought Christina, is being a friend to Dolly. How can I be Dolly's friend when she listens to Mr. Shevvington, not me?

Jonah pulled ahead. Two tenth-grade boys spun by Christina as easily as birds on the wing. Jonah called back over his shoulder, "Hey, Christina, you wanna come over to my house? Have something hot to drink? My toes are freezing off."

"Hot date!" shouted the tenth-graders. "What an invitation — his toes are freezing off! You gonna warm 'em up, Christina?" One of them swiped at Christina, knocking off her cap. Her hair spilled out, blowing in the relentless winter wind.

A true friend, Christina thought, is a person who

helps even when the friendship isn't close anymore. "You're jealous, aren't you?" she said. How nice to call somebody *else* jealous.

The wind separated the strands of her hair: silver and gold, chocolate laced. The tenth-grader grinned and slowed down. They skated in step: her right leg swirling across the ice in tempo with his, then left legs together and right again. When his hand reached toward her hair, Christina knew he was not going to yank it, the way seventh-grade boys would. "I love your hair," said the boy softly. "Silver and gold and brown. It's — "

Jonah skated between them.

The huge clumpy feet he tripped over in class were graceful in long, black, men's skates.

Jonah said firmly, "Leave it alone."

Jonah's mother acted as if Christina came every afternoon. They made hot chocolate in a big, friendly, messy kitchen, with Jonah's little sister swinging her legs from the counter and Jonah's little brother yelling because it was his turn to sort the laundry. They played Monopoly on the table, and Mrs. Bergeron hardly noticed when chocolate got spilled on a Community Chest. There were dripping winter boots and newspapers sliding off their stacks; school books tumbling into the unsorted laundry; and between Monopoly turns they all investigated the freezer for things to microwave.

It was like her own home, cluttered with love and talk.

Christina bit into a sugar cookie, and suddenly

she was so homesick she wanted to weep. She could actually taste home: a taste of crunchy sweetness, of cookies still hot from the oven.

Jonah walked Christina home because it had grown dark. She felt the way she might after Thanksgiving dinner: stuffed. But with friendship, instead of turkey. Jonah's mother had said to come back anytime.

Can I come back to live? she wanted to beg. Can I stay with you? I'll sleep in the hall, I'll sleep standing up — oh, please let me live here instead of at Schooner Inne! But of course she didn't. She said, "Thank you, I will."

And when Jonah said good-bye on the steps of the Schooner Inne, and she went inside all alone, it was truly a temperature change. The chill of loneliness lowered Christina's resistance. All her fears lived here, and none of her allies.

In the gloomy front hall, where the slender white railings twirled up and up toward the black cupola, she remembered her slumber party and the game of murder. In the dark, she thought, there will be an accident.

After all, little girls get silly. Would it be surprising if one toppled off the balcony onto her spine? The Shevvingtons would be absolved of all blame. People would feel sorry for them and bring casseroles and potted plants.

Chapter 10

Mrs. Shevvington rented a charming, antique maid's costume for Anya. It was a long, black cotton dress with a starched lacy white apron and cap. "That's sick," cried Christina. "You should make her wear school clothes and go back to school. Not dress her like a maid!"

"She's happy, Christina," said Michael irritably.

"I think she looks pretty neat," Benjamin added. This was amazing. Benj never expressed the slightest interest in girls or their looks.

Christina tried to explain her point to the Jayes. Benjamin, Michael, and Dolly Jaye frowned at Christina, an impenetrable family unit.

Mr. Shevvington said sadly, "Can't you rejoice when poor Anya has a moment of pleasure? Must you always keep happiness for yourself?" He put an arm around the trio of Jayes and the other arm over Anya's black shoulder.

Christina, the outsider, flushed.

Benj and Michael teased their little sister, told her to have fun, and dashed out before the guests arrived. The girls came in a clump, giggling and pushing. Including Gretchen and Vicki; Katy, who never got invited anywhere; and Dolly, who wasn't in seventh grade at all.

The first game Mrs. Shevvington organized was Pin the Tail On The Donkey.

"Mrs. Shevvington," protested Gretch, laughing. "Nobody's played that since they were little. That's a baby game."

"Ah," said Mrs. Shevvington, "but we need to be in a certain order, and however well you do in *this* game is the order in which you will enter the second game."

Christina was not surprised when Gretch won, Dolly came in second, and Vicki third. She was not surprised when Mrs. Shevvington lined up the girls in order of winning, so that fat Katy was marked the loser, last in line, while Dolly stood up front, between Gretch and Vicki.

"Everybody pair up now!" ordered Mrs. Shevvington. "Next game is in pairs!"

"I get to play with Gretchen!" cried Dolly joyfully. She beamed at Gretchen, who said to her, "I love your red hair, Dolly. And your name! It's so sweet. You are sort of a dolly." Gretchen and Dolly held hands and talked about dancing class.

Christina stood with Katy. We're the losers, she thought.

She gave Mrs. Shevvington the dirtiest look she could. Mrs. Shevvington said loudly, "Why, Christina! As hostess I expect you to make sure *every* guest has a good time. Are you complaining about your partner?"

Poor Katy bit her lips and stumbled. Her plain face turned splotchy red and her eyes welled up with unshed tears.

Dinner was wonderful: huge platters of lasagna, soft hot rolls with sweet butter, and salad for greenery. "Nobody is actually required to eat any salad, of course," said Mr. Shevvington, smiling down at the girls, "because this is a fun time, and we want even vegetable haters to have fun all night long." The girls applauded Mr. Shevvington, who bowed and escorted each girl into the formal dining room. During dinner Mr. Shevvington told wonderful scary stories about the sea captain who built the house and his bride, who flung herself to a horrible death from the cupola of this very house, exactly one hundred years before. "Tonight, when it's dark," he whispered, "I'll tell you what happened to the sea captain after his wife vanished in the terrible tides of Candle Cove."

Gretch and Vicki screamed with delight. "Horror stories!" shouted Vicki. "I love them."

"You are one," muttered Katy.

Christina laughed for the first time that night. Katy had potential.

After supper they popped popcorn and made caramel popcorn balls. They sang crazy songs — the sort with twenty verses you learn in summer camp. Mrs. Shevvington had them play Charades of brand names. Gretch did Wrangler jeans; Vicki got Coca-

Cola; Dolly got Burger King. Mrs. Shevvington explained that Christina would go last, because the guests always came ahead of the hostess. Then, when it was finally Christina's turn and she was aching to act, Mrs. Shevvington said everybody was bored now, and they would do something else.

Mr. Shevvington looked across the popcorn at his wife. Mrs. Shevvington looked back. Their smiles seemed to fit in midair like a key and a lock. Their eyes slid around the room and landed on Dolly. Dolly was sitting between Gretch and Vicki. Vicki was feeding Dolly a popcorn ball, Vicki holding it, Dolly nibbling. Gretch talked about Dolly as if she really *were* a doll. "Isn't she adorable?" giggled Gretch.

"She's so sweet," agreed Vicki, stroking Dolly's braids as though she had just purchased Dolly in a department store.

Dolly preened.

"We're going to play," said Mr. Shevvington softly. *"Murder."*

The girls all screamed joyfully.

"Now you must listen to the rules very carefully. Especially the first one. This is a big house and a scary one. You must not go into the cellar. Is that absolutely clear? Everybody repeat the promise. 'I will not go into the cellar.' "

They all promised.

There is something down there, Christina thought. They don't mind if I am trapped by the thing. They don't mind if it comes and goes from the school and the cellar. But they mind if people like Gretch and Vicki find out.

"Next rule," said Mrs. Shevvington. Her eyes never left Dolly. She was smiling, her little corn teeth lying between her thin lips. "You will all hide in pairs." She was breathing heavily, excited about things to come.

Christina thought how the stairs narrowed on the third floor and the balcony tilted. "If we hide in pairs," Christina shouted, "I want to be Dolly's partner."

"No way," said Gretch, irked. "She belongs to me."

"I'm with Gretchen," Dolly agreed. "You stay with Katy, Christina."

Katy hung her head. "You don't have to stay with me, Christina," she murmured. "You can find somebody else."

Mrs. Shevvington looked at Christina. Every girl at the party could read that expression. Really, Christina — can't you be nice to that poor, ugly, little fat girl for one evening?

They've won a round, Christina thought. They're making me look like the bad guy when *they're* the bad guys. "They'll never find *us*, Katy," said Christina. "I know all the best spots in the house. Stick with me! We'll get that Murderer." She lifted her chin, staring into Mr. Shevvington's eyes, blue tonight. But Mr. Shevvington looked youthful and innocent, as if all he had in mind was a silly game in a silly house with silly girls.

But Mrs. Shevvington's lips curled, like an animal preparing to eat raw meat. It's her, Christina thought. She's the dangerous one.

Mr. Shevvington explained the complex rules of Murder. They had to keep on the move, avoid being killed, and yet find out who the killer was. They had to stay with their partners. They could not get in large groups.

Mr. Shevvington put a cassette into the stereo and flipped the switch, which played the music in every room. The slithering strings of violins trembled in the air like old ghosts.

Mrs. Shevvington turned out the lights.

The guests scattered through the house, banging their shins on furniture. The stairs creaked as they dashed up and down. Crazy giggles ricocheted like bullets.

In the dark, Christina could watch nobody. Katy held so tight to her hand Christina thought her bones might break.

Wherever it would happen, it would happen up high in the mansion. So Christina dragged Katy up the first flight of stairs and then up the second. "I don't wanna be up here," Katy wailed. "It's too scary up here."

"Sssssshhh," Christina said.

"Let's hide under the dining-room table, Chrissie," Katy whispered.

"Shut up," Christina hissed.

The house began to fill with screams as heavy hands and cold fingers unexpectedly touched a player in the dark.

Then the girls began screaming just for the fun of it. Somebody turned the eerie violins up higher.

Anya began screaming for real: the ghastly high scream Christina remembered so well. Once, screaming like that, Anya had tried to step out the third-floor window, seeing fire where there was only fog.

Anya screamed like an animal. Christina imagined Anya frozen with fear in the dark. Was Anya to be the victim, not Dolly? Had the Shevvingtons seen Anya's improvement after all? Was playing with Dolly just intended to confuse Christina?

"Chrissie! Chrissie! Chrissie, where are you?" screamed Anya.

Once Anya's fears had pulled her to the edge of the cliffs. Now — during the slumber party — was something pushing her instead?

"I'm coming, Anya!" She abandoned Katy, racing in the blackness down the stairs. "Stand still, Anya, so I can find you. It's all right, it's just a game; don't be afraid."

"Christina, shut up!" Gretch yelled from some other location. "You're ruining the game. Let her scream. It's wonderful. She has the best scream of all."

Christina felt her way into the kitchen, to the source of the screams. "I'm here, Anya." Christina edged forward. A white splotch appeared in the dark. Anya was only inches away. Christina reached for the lace trim on the apron.

Too late, Christina heard the giggle.

She caught desperately at the wall, at chairs, at

anything — but there was nothing to hold.

The giggle turned into a groan.

The white vanished. The dark turned into a black hole.

And it was Christina who fell. Down the cellar stairs. Hitting the steps, hitting the rail, hitting the stone floor.

Down into the waiting giggle.

Chapter 11

Morning sun glittered on new-fallen snow.

The snow had blown into wonderful drifts, like whorls on top of a lemon meringue pie.

Christina's knees hurt. She stumbled to school.

Jonah came running to meet her. "What happened, Christina?" he asked. "I know Mondays are pretty bad — but limping?"

Gretch and Vicki bounded up. "We had the best slumber party ever!" cried Gretch. "They live in the most wonderful house. You should just see all the treasures. Mr. and Mrs. Shevvington are so terrific to those island children. We should all be so lucky. We had the best food and the best fun. I got to sleep in a bed with its own little stepstool because the mattress was so high: me and Dolly and Vicki. It was perfect."

"I was asking about Christina's limp," Jonah said, turning his back on Gretch.

Gretch and Vicki threw back their heads and howled with laughter. "When we played Murder, Mr. Shevvington said the only rule was, 'Don't go near the cellar.' So who goes into the cellar? Christina!"

Jonah knew Christina's cellar stories. He knew she would never have gone into the cellar again in her life. Jonah put a brotherly arm around her and said, "Chrissie, are you all right?"

It was comfort, not romance, but Vicki and Gretch were furious with jealousy. "She just skinned her knees," said Vicki, brushing it off. "Anyhow it was her own fault. She opened the bolt on the cellar door herself."

"I did not!" cried Christina. "The door was wide open when I got there! I was trying to save Anya."

"Save Anya?" they repeated. Vicki and Gretch fell on each other, laughing. "Christina, it was a game. Nobody needed saving. We were all having a good time screaming. Anya's elevator doesn't go all the way to the top anyhow, you know. Her mind melted last year. Only the world's best shrink could save her now."

Christina was trembling. "Somebody opened the cellar door on purpose, Jonah."

"Oh, right," Vicki said. "You're always trying to blame somebody, Christina Romney. You tell people you have this terrible life, but it's all lies. The Shevvingtons are fabulous. And no matter how rotten you are to your guests, like poor Katy, and no matter how demanding you are and how you try to force Dolly into stuff — the Shevvingtons forgive you and try to help you. Now you're even trying to blame somebody else because you went and opened the cellar door, which you're not allowed to do." They flounced away.

Jonah asked, "Did you fall, Chrissie? Or were you pushed?"

He believes me, Christina thought.

At the party not even Anya had believed her!

She had felt the thing's fingers on her skin. They were cold, and they stank of the sea. It was like being stroked by a fish.

But the crash of her body on the stairs had saved her. The noise brought Katy, Jennie, Amanda, and Linda running. The slimy fingers retreated to the shadows in the back of the cellar. Christina lay in a crumpled pile at the bottom of the rickety stairs.

Every guest at the party gathered in the door to tell her what an idiot she was, falling down the steps in her own house.

"Jonah," Christina whispered now. "It was there. It's real. It lives. It touched me." Everything granite in Christina disintegrated. She put her arms around Jonah, hung her troubles around his neck, and wept.

But they were too young, and it was too soon. Jonah was appalled. His friends would see; it was too intimate; they were in public; what was she doing? He forgot the cellar and the giggle and the Shevvingtons and pulled back, trying to disassociate himself from all that affection and need. "I — um — I'll see you in — uh — class," he said desperately. "And — I'm busy this afternoon — I — I hope your knees are okay." And he fled.

Christina snapped an icicle off the row that lined the school and threw it like a tiny javelin into a drift of snow. When she turned around, Jonah, Vicki, and Gretchen had disappeared. Christina stood alone.

It was seventeen below. The cold chewed her fingers. By the time the last warning bell rang and she forced herself into the building, her fingers were stiff and blue.

In homeroom they had to fill out forms for state-wide testing, which would take place later in the month. When she tried to write, the letters came out looking like Egyptian hieroglyphics. My mind feels like that, thought Christina. Meaningless curves and twitches.

The day passed in a similar fashion, twitching and curving.

Who was the next victim of the Shevvingtons? Did they want Dolly or Anya or Christina? Who was the thing? What did *he* want?

"The essay," said Mrs. Shevvington in English class, "is to write a contemporary parallel of a fairy tale. I will assign the fairy tale. Jonah, for example, will have *The Little Red Hen*. In this story, of course, no farm animal will help the little red hen raise the wheat or grind the flour, but when the loaves are baked, they all want to eat it. The moral, of course, is that if you want to enjoy the results you must put in the work first."

Mrs. Shevvington circled the room. She stopped at Katy's desk and smiled at Katy. Christina knew that smile. She tried to think how to stand between fat, ugly Katy and that smile, but no solution came to her. "I'm hoping to make each story match the student," Mrs. Shevvington said to the class. "That way it will be more fun."

Fun for whom? wondered Christina.

Katy must have had the same thought. She gathered herself, ready for the blows.

"You, Katy," said Mrs. Shevvington, the smile growing like a blister on her skin, "will do the story of the ugly duckling."

Katy went so white the pimples stood out on her face like a rash.

Gretchen and Vicki giggled.

Mrs. Shevvington turned to Christina.

Die, you hateful woman, Christina thought, willing Mrs. Shevvington to have a heart attack.

Mrs. Shevvington simply smiled wider. "Christina, you will update the story of the boy who cried wolf." Her little teeth lay between her thin lips like pellets from an air gun. "Of course in the new version, it will be the *girl* who cried wolf."

The class had expected something that would make Christina cry. This was nothing. They were disappointed.

But Christina understood. The message was very clear.

You may scream for help all you want, Christina, my dear. Nobody will believe you. And then, when you really need help, when the screams are loud and real — no one will come, Christina of the Isle. You are alone.

Chapter 12

It used to be that the ending of school was a clock thing: the big hand on twelve and the little hand on three. But now the close of school was a physical relief of body and soul. I'm out. It's over for a while.

"Everybody's coming over to my house," said Jonah. "Want to come, Chrissie?"

Benjamin bounded by, headed for his garage job. Suddenly it struck Christina that Benj was still in high school, though he had always planned to quit at sixteen.

How clever the Shevvingtons were. Benjamin and Michael Jaye were the balance. If anybody noticed that right after Anya fell apart, Dolly developed strange fears and Christina behaved oddly — why, Mr. Shevvington could point out how successfully he had kept this fine young lobsterman in school.

"Yes, I'm coming," said Christina.

Across the school yard Dolly flew, her new jeans so long that the rolled cuffs made pale blue saucers around her skinny ankles. "Chrissie?" she called.

Her voice was as thin as a snow flurry.

Traitor, thought Christina. Her eyes stung with hot tears that Dolly should have joined up with Gretchen and Vicki and the Shevvingtons.

"Chrissie, don't be mad."

Christina turned her back on Dolly to go with Jonah.

"Chrissie, I need you," Dolly said.

They were Christina Romney's words. Her love of helping people was as strong as her love of life itself.

"Chrissie, dancing class is so scary. I'm in the advanced class, but I'm not as good as the advanced girls. I have to dance alone, and they laugh at me. I've begged the Shevvingtons, but they won't let me drop out. They say it's good for me to face some competition for a change. They say on the island we didn't know anything about the real world." Her pixie face was turned up into Christina's, waiting for Christina to solve her problem.

A very heavy hand landed on Christina's shoulder. Mrs. Shevvington had materialized. Her candle-stub fingers pressed painfully between the bones of Christina's shoulder, and then attached themselves to Dolly's head. "You must try your very best," said Mrs. Shevvington to Dolly.

Dolly's tiny diamond-shaped faced was skewed by grief. "My best," said Dolly, "isn't good enough."

The Shevvingtons do not destroy by any evil of our times, thought Christina. Not by drugs, not by alcohol. But by an evil as ancient as time: cutting

away strength, beauty, confidence, friendship —
until there is nothing left, just a shell.

"Dolly, that's wonderful!" cried Mrs. Shevvington. "I'm so proud of you! If you get nothing else
out of dancing class, you've learned a very important lesson. Sometimes your best just isn't enough,
and you have to accept being ordinary. You island
girls oft times have difficulty admitting your ordi-
nariness. You are so sure you are special."

Dolly's red hair seemed duller, her fair skin wan-
ner, her bright eyes dimmer.

Mrs. Shevvington smiled. "You run along to your
class now, Dolly."

Dolly obeyed instantly, like a slave, like —
like Anya.

In Jonah's yard the snow was thigh high. Jonah
brought out snow shovels and brooms. The children
shoveled paths. He had drawn a maze on paper and
was shouting directions, but nobody listened, shoveling joyfully at their own routes. The paths inter-
locked and dead-ended. White walls of shoveled
snow grew higher and higher, until only the fluffy
pompons on their ski caps showed above the passage
walls.

Above their heads, the sun set in a sky the color
of frostbite. Pink channels appeared in the heavens
as if dead children frolicked there in a maze of pearl.

Jonah's mother leaned out the back door. "Getting late, kids!" she called. "All you who have to be
home before dark, set out now!"

Christina hoped Jonah would offer to walk her

home, but he was too busy finishing the maze. When she called good-bye, he hardly glanced up.

Don't cry, Christina told herself. You had a great afternoon. Shoveling snow with your friends. Maybe I want too much. Maybe I have to learn to enjoy less instead of craving more.

She did not want to go back to Schooner Inne.

From Jonah's she went the long way, staring at front doors, wishing she could board with anybody but the Shevvingtons. She passed a phone booth and thought of telephoning her mother and saying, Mommy come get me. Come understand. She passed the laundromat, where Anya presumably stood in the hot, humid air, emptying detergent into washers. She went to the harbor, where the few boats in the water were crusted with ice.

High above her on the opposite cliff loomed Schooner Inne, cold and white as ice. A wisp of smoke drifted up from behind the roof of Schooner Inne. Christina could not remember the Shevvingtons lighting a fire before. Christina wanted to warm her blue fingers at that fire and stare into the flames, a comfort as old as mankind.

She ran up Breakneck Hill.

Mr. Shevvington opened the door for her. He did not speak. His face was hard and cold as the winter sky. Gripping her shoulders, he yanked Christina through the long hall with its flocked emerald paper and the staircase rising like a wedding cake. Michael and Benj were standing there; she stumbled past, her feet catching on their big winter boots, and they did nothing. They might have been framed photographs on the wall. Dolly was on the second step, making a mustache of her braids, staring at Christina.

Mr. Shevvington pushed her ahead of him, into the kitchen. For a moment she thought he was going to lock her in the cellar, and she came close to screaming. But he opened the back door. He's throwing me out, thought Christina, numb with confusion.

Mr. Shevvington held Christina in front of him as if preparing her for a firing squad. She felt smaller than Dolly: little-girl weak.

"Look at that!" said Mr. Shevvington through gritted teeth.

Spirals of fire shot like gold silk into the air.

A bonfire in the snow.

"You put your entire wardrobe on that fire!" said Mr. Shevvington. "All your clothes, Christina. You set fire to them."

"She warned us," said Mrs. Shevvington. "We have to admit that. She even wrote an essay and insisted on reading it aloud to the class, detailing how she would dispose of all her possessions in a fire."

"I didn't, either," cried Christina. "You made me read that out loud. You know I didn't really mean it. It was your assignment."

"It was your January daydream," said Mrs. Shevvington. She jabbed a poker into the fire. In the ashes Christina recognized her snowflake sweater. It *is* my clothing, she thought. "I would never do that. I was at Jonah's all afternoon," she said desperately.

"On the contrary, Christina. You left Jonah's house an hour ago. I telephoned his mother. You sneaked into Schooner Inne, got your wardrobe, found matches and a can of oil from the cellar you so love to explore, and set this fire. Then you ran away to the harbor so you could return later and pretend to be innocent."

Mr. Shevvington shoveled snow to smother the fire. It hissed.

The loss of her clothing became real. She had nothing to wear. The presents of Christmas, only a month ago: gone. Burned. Her mother's hand-knit sweaters. The memories of their shopping together in the distant city for school clothes.

Mr. Shevvington took Christina's shoulder, roughly hauling her back into the kitchen.

What will my mother say? Christina thought. Tears spilled from her eyes, hit her cold hands, and spattered on the floor.

She looked at Michael, whom she had loved the first twelve years of her life and wanted to marry, so they could live happily ever after on the island. Michael avoided her eyes.

She looked at Benj, who had been the older brother for them all: organized the games, been the referee, the baby-sitter, or sandwich maker. Benj stared at the ceiling.

She looked at Dolly, and Dolly looked steadily back. "Chrissie," she said. "Mrs. Shevvington explained to me how jealous you are because I have new clothes and you don't. Because I have dancing lessons and you don't. Because I'm happy here and you aren't. If I had known you were going to start setting fires to get attention, Chrissie, I — "

"I did not!" cried Christina. "How could you think that, Dolly? You know I would never do a thing like that."

Dolly frowned. "But Christina," she said patiently, "the Shevvingtons said so." Dolly, Michael, and Benjamin Jaye nodded in unison. *The Shevvingtons said so.*

"That doesn't mean it's true," Christina whispered.

Dolly, Michael, and Benj looked at her reproachfully. The room echoed with their thoughts. *The Shevvingtons said so.*

Christina sat down before she fell over. "Where's Anya?" she said. Her mouth felt thick, as if the dentist had just given her a shot before filling a cavity.

"She's resting," said Mrs. Shevvington sharply. "You are not to disturb her. Naturally, she is very frightened by this. You know how fragile Anya is, Christina. No matter how selfish you are, no matter how determined to spoil things and terrify others, I truly thought you had enough concern for Anya to protect her. Clearly I was wrong. You will do anything for attention."

Mr. and Mrs. Shevvington telephoned Christina's parents.

They gave their version of the fire first.

How clever they were. "Of course you tried so hard," said Mrs. Shevvington sympathetically. "It's terribly difficult to deal with an adolescent. How could you have known you were spoiling Christina so badly in your effort to give her a good life?"

Christina wanted to rip the telephone out of their hands, but she restrained herself. It would not help.

"Christina in her terrible jealousy," said Mrs. Shevvington in the gentlest voice in the world, "was forced to extremes to get attention. Her mental and emotional state is very unfortunate. I'm so sad about it, Mrs. Romney. We want you to know that Mr. Shevvington and I will help you in every way. When families are hit by tragedies like this, they must be brave."

Christina touched her hair. Sometimes she could actually feel its colors — the silver and gold like ribbons of honor spun through the brown. Tonight she could feel nothing. She was running out of courage.

"Christina needs serious professional help," said Mr. Shevvington when it was his turn. How soft his voice was. Velvet.

This is how they finished Val off, thought Christina. They got her parents to put her in a mental institution. *Would my parents abandon me like that?*

Mrs. Shevvington handed Christina the telephone. The little black holes in the middle of her eyes looked like the black hole of the cellar.

"I'd like to speak to my parents privately, please," said Christina. She was reaching bottom.

If she did, the Shevvingtons would win. She imagined them going into her bedroom, emptying her bureau drawers, taking blouses off hangers, keeping Michael and Benj and Dolly away from windows. Setting that fire.

I know the truth, she thought, but that doesn't matter. The truth by itself is nothing. You have to be able to convince other people or it doesn't count. Christina took a deep breath. "Mommy?" she said. "Daddy? It isn't true. They're making it up."

Her mother was sobbing. The sobs continued all through Christina's talking. Her father was breathing deeply, as if he were in a tennis match. "Are they making it up, Chrissie?" said her father sadly. "There was a fire, wasn't there? And your clothing on it?"

"Daddy, I didn't put it there! The Shevvingtons did! It's part of a plot they have."

"Oh, dear God," said her mother, who never swore, who would only say that as a prayer. "Mr. Shevvington is right. That is true paranoia. Believing you are surrounded by evil plots! Chrissie, darling. Mommy loves you, do you believe that?"

"Yes, I believe it!" cried Christina. "I always believe you! It's your turn to believe me. That essay was an assignment. But it gave them a clue about how to get me. I know Mr. Shevvington is the high-school principal, but he's the one who is insane. Just because you're a teacher doesn't mean you're a good person. Don't you remember what happened to Anya? It's part of their plan. I'm next, you see!"

She turned to her audience at the Inne, to see

the effect of her speech on them. Benj and Michael looked incredibly sad. Benj — strong, tough Benj — had tears in his eyes.

It has worked, thought Christina. They think I'm crazy. This is how it worked with Val. I never knew how they pulled it off, but when you are the authority, it's easy.

Mrs. Shevvington's silver tongue had done its evil work.

To every protest Christina made, her parents replied, *But the Shevvingtons said so.* "Mommy," said Christina over and over again, "Mommy, believe me." But her mother did not.

Chapter 13

Several years before Michael and Benj had been fascinated by torture. They loved reading about the gruesome things man had done to man. Michael's favorite torture was Assyrian: the warriors slowly slit their prisoners' skin away. Benj's favorite was from Merrie Olde Englande, where they would chain the prisoner to a rock by the sea and let the tide rise up to drown him inch by inch.

As the whole seventh grade shunned her (that creepy girl from that creepy island, setting fire to her own clothes) she wondered which was more horrible. Physical torture or psychological?

· There was only one day of school before her parents' arrival on the mainland. It lasted as long as the thirteen years of her life.

Only Jonah stuck by her — and for that, nobody would associate with him either. "What really happened?" Gretch asked viciously in the cafeteria.

"The Shevvingtons did it," Christina said. The teacher on cafeteria duty was shocked; Christina could already hear the report on her insanity.

"They're grown-ups," Gretchen said. "They wouldn't set fire to your clothes. It's sick."

Christina imagined her parents' visit. They'd take her shopping (with money they could not spare) for a new, plain, serviceable wardrobe. Three pairs of Brand X jeans, socks that came six in a plastic package. Even the clothes would be a punishment. "The Shevvingtons are sick," said Christina.

But of course nobody accepted this. They all loved the Shevvingtons.

Only Katy, whom Mrs. Shevvington routinely whipped, and Robbie, who had lost his sister Val, believed. But Katy and Robbie were Nobody. To be believed, you had to have the support of the Somebodies.

"Maybe Anya did it," said Katy, trying to find an acceptable "out" for Christina.

The children and teacher considered this and were willing to believe it.

If I let them blame Anya, thought Christina, I will be safe. I will have friends again. Nobody will get me "professional help" like Val.

How she wanted to blame Anya. Why not use Anya for that? What good was Anya anyway? She could hardly even keep a job folding clothes.

But if I let them blame Anya, thought Christina, I will be even more evil than the Shevvingtons. She straightened, knowing she would never have a friend again. Maybe not even Jonah. "It was the Shevvingtons," she said. "Anya would never do that."

They stepped back from her. Gretchen chewed

on a ribbon of her thin hair. "If it wasn't Anya," said Gretch, smiling, "then . . . it was you."

In the middle of science came a summons for Christina to go to the office to see Mr. Shevvington. The class snickered. "Here it comes," they said. "He'll lock you up, Chrissie. You'll have shrinks from here to Texas."

Cheeks scarlet, heart ice, Christina stood up and walked alone to the principal's office. The metal lockers on each side of the hall were like prison doors, opening and slamming, row on row. What was it like for Val? Was Val scared all the time? Did Val whimper and beg? Did Val even know?

Mr. Shevvington was wearing a charcoal suit with gray pinstripes, a vest, and a crimson tie. He looked like a diplomat on his way to catch a plane somewhere important. The secretaries at their desks and two mothers waiting in the office looked at him with adoration.

"Christina, dear," he said. "We need to have a little chat about counseling." He sounded so caring. The secretaries and the mothers smiled, happy that he loved the strange, sick little island girl.

Christina said nothing. The mothers were Vicki's and Gretchen's mothers. He had brought her down here on purpose to display her to them!

Mr. Shevvington hugged her. She wanted to throw up. But if she showed how she felt, it would be a mark against her, not him. So she pretended to be comfortable. "I want to be sure you aren't upset or anxious, Chrissie, honey."

They beamed at his understanding support of a little girl.

"Chrissie, sweetie," said Mr. Shevvington, ruffling her hair.

"Don't call me Chrissie," she said hotly. She flattened her hair back down the way it belonged. She took three steps away and glared at him. "I am not anxious. I do not intend to have counseling."

The mothers looked at her reprovingly. The secretaries exchanged resigned shrugs.

Mr. Shevvington coaxed, "I bought a new rock tape I know you'll enjoy."

"No, thank you," Christina said. "I have to get back to class." She lifted her chin and exited. She was so filled with fury she paused right outside the office, leaning against the wall, wanting to go back and slug him.

The conversation continued, and she heard it perfectly.

"Ungrateful little thing, isn't she, Mr. Shevvington?" said Vicki's mother. "It's so generous of you to take care of these island children. We all have the greatest respect for you and Mrs. Shevvington, putting up with their shenanigans. I know Michael Jaye is an asset to the basketball team, but the *rest* of them! Frightening little monsters!"

"That Anya practically threw her boyfriend off the cliff last fall. Why, Blake's parents had to ship him off to boarding school to keep him safe," said Gretch's mother. "And this Christina child! You should hear the stories my daughter brings home about Christina."

"That hair's weird, don't you think?" said a secretary. "Those three colors, like a painted flag? She's stained. *Marked.*"

Christina could hardly breathe from shame and rage.

She remembered the September morning when she and Anya, Michael, and Benj had stood among the tourists on Frankie's boat, headed for the mainland and the first day of school. The tourists had whispered about Christina's three-colored hair and Anya's chalk-white countenance. *"They look like ancient island princesses. Marked out for sacrifice. Sent away for the sake of the islanders, to be given to the sea."*

Had it been a prophecy? Was it coming true?

But Mr. Shevvington laughed. "Now, ladies. Christina is a difficult child, but she chooses to be. It is not a result of her unattractive hair."

Christina almost put her fist through the cement block wall. I have beautiful hair!

"You must love teaching," one mother said to Mr. Shevvington.

"Yes, indeed. I think of each class as a zoo." He laughed. "Twenty-six to a cage."

We are animals to the Shevvingtons, thought Christina.

The mothers matched chuckle with chuckle.

"Mrs. Shevvington and I are very fond of the island children, for all their flaws," said Mr. Shevvington. "We're taking them all skiing over the next three-day weekend. You know how isolated those island children are. Not one of them has ever been

100

on skis. Isn't that amazing? In Maine? We're trying to broaden their horizons a little bit."

"Mr. Shevvington, how generous of you! Downhill skiing? Lift passes, ski rentals, ski lodges, and everything?"

"Of course," said Mr. Shevvington.

Christina could actually *hear* his smile. It had a stretched, false sound.

"Little Dolly Jaye has a fear of heights," Mr. Shevvington said lovingly. "I thought we would cure her of it in the most delightful way. We've bought her a darling little ski outfit. I can hardly wait to see Dolly going down the slopes at full speed, all her fears behind her."

And what accident, Christina thought, do you want her to have in front of you?

She might never have a friend again, but she still had a mother and father. Her parents' visit was wonderful. They made no mention of the fire, the weeping phone calls, or the expense of new clothes.

Refusing the Shevvingtons' offer of a guest room at Schooner Inne, Mr. and Mrs. Romney drove to Boston to a huge city hotel. Christina sat squashed in the front seat between her parents, her father's hand on her knee, her mother's kisses on her cheek.

They went to the Children's Museum and the Science Museum; they all played the strange games and tests at the Computer Museum. They hiked the historic walks and talked of Paul Revere and John Hancock.

At night they sat in an enormous lounge, where

the pianist played long, slow, soothing pieces, and a waiter in black tails brought trays of steaming hot snacks.

Her mother and father told the island gossip — who was mad at whom, who was late paying the oil bill, whose kids were shaping up to be good at basketball. After supper they went to a late movie she had yearned to see but the Shevvingtons had said was too "mature" for her.

"It wasn't very mature," said Christina afterward. "Just violent."

When they went shopping, instead of the plain sweater Christina had expected, they found two lovely shaker knits: one peach, one so green and foresty that Christina knew Dolly would want to borrow it. Her father found a sweatsuit of bright yellow with orange parrots floating among lime green leaves. It made her feel safe as summer and lemonade.

Her father gave her more spending money than she had ever had at one time, all in new, crisp one-dollar bills, so she felt like an executive, with a real wad of money. "I like that word, *wad*," she told her father. They measured the bills across, and it was really nice and thick and waddy.

Christina knew she was safe. It was time to tell the truth. "We have to sort out what's been happening at Schooner Inne," said Christina. She thought, They will rescue me somehow. And Dolly and Anya. I won't need the proof in the briefcase, just my own mother and father. I should have known that all along.

"Chrissie," said her parents. "No matter what happens, we will stand by you."

Ice touched Christina's heart. "What happened was something Mr. and Mrs. Shevvington did," she said.

They looked at her sadly. "Christina, at some point a person must take responsibility for her own actions. You cannot blame the Shevvingtons for Anya's mental collapse. You cannot blame the Shevvingtons that Dolly is afraid of heights or doing poorly in dancing class. And sweetie, you cannot blame the Shevvingtons for your own uncontrollable rages."

Christina could not believe this! All their cuddling and shopping meant nothing! They were on the Shevvington's side! They too, like Michael and Benj and Dolly, thought if the Shevvingtons said so, then it was so. "If somebody accused *you* of bad things," she cried, "I would know they were lying, no matter how much proof there was."

Her parents talked gently of counseling, of telephoning every single night to keep in touch, no matter what the cost of the calls out to sea. Their talk was like the sea itself, lapping away at the shore.

Her father wiped away her tears with the flat of his big, thick thumbs, and her mother rocked her. "Try to stay calm, darling. See if you can last until vacation. If it's still bad, I'll rent an apartment in the village, and we'll live together."

Christina wanted to scream *Yes, yes, yes, do that!*

But her mother and father would be separated.

He on the island, she on shore. She would have to close down the tiny restaurant that supported them through the winter. They would have to admit to the islanders, as Anya's parents had before them, that her daughter could not survive on the mainland. They had splurged on this lovely weekend as a way of saying, We love you. They would also pay a second rent to say, We love you.

But it was Christina's task to say, No, I'm fine, don't worry about it, it'll all work out. So she said it. "No, I'm fine now," she told her parents. She hated her words. They sounded like an admission that she had burned her clothes. But some of the lines on her father's face smoothed away, and her mother's cheeks seemed pinker. So Christina did not say to them, the Shevvingtons are going to take us to a ski resort! They are going to get Dolly there! Instead she said softly, "Don't worry about it."

Now more than ever, what the Shevvingtons had planned must be stopped. For her own sake . . . for Dolly . . . for Anya . . . for her mother and father.

Chapter 14

In English, an amazing thing happened. Mrs. Shevvington picked on Gretchen. This had never happened before.

The essay was to be about the most precious possession in your household — perhaps a baby photograph or an old dish of a grandmother's, a cherished wedding present. Mrs. Shevvington had Gretchen read aloud.

"The most precious thing in my house," read Gretchen proudly, "is my private telephone line." She knew she was the only person in the seventh grade with her own phone book listing. "I have three different phones I can plug into the jack. My favorite is an Elvis phone. It — "

"I beg your pardon," said Mrs. Shevvington, sparse eyebrows raised contemptuously. "Are you saying that *the sound of your own voice* is your most precious possession?"

The class laughed at Gretchen. She was not used to it. She stumbled. "No — I — um — it's the phone I like."

"Oh. I see," said Mrs. Shevvington in that cruel, silken voice. "So that all your admirers can reach you?"

Gretchen turned beet red. She looked ill.

"Nobody else listed herself as the most precious object," said Mrs. Shevvington. "I'm fascinated, Gretchen. I don't know which is more interesting. That you consider yourself an object, or that you consider the sound of your voice so magnificent."

Gretchen's essay pages shivered in the air. The meaner boys — the boys Gretchen herself had trained to do this — began flapping their arms to match her shaking hand.

"Try to be less self-centered, Gretchen," said Mrs. Shevvington. Mrs. Shevvington sat calmly, her thick body like a piece of the desk, her oatmeal face solid. "Think of another subject."

The mean people leaned back and smirked. Gretchen was as exposed as if she had been stripped of clothing.

"Well?" said Mrs. Shevvington.

Gretchen was now white as kindergarten paste.

"I can't think of anything," mumbled Gretchen. "My head is empty."

Empty, thought Christina. Mrs. Shevvington had emptied her. Just for today, of course. Nothing permanent, like Val.

A minute passed. The big old school clock made a slight tick as the minute hand twitched and moved on. Gretchen stood hot and stupid in front of the class. Even Vicki did nothing. Gretchen had not a friend in the world.

Christina knew how that felt. "If I had an Elvis phone," said Christina, "I would list it first, too, Mrs. Shevvington. I don't think it's fair of you to decide what is important to other people."

She had truly caught Mrs. Shevvington by surprise. "I do not think I was addressing you, Christina Romney," said Mrs. Shevvington.

"No, I don't think you were either, Mrs. Shevvington. But I would like to hear about the other two telephones. Could you read the rest of your essay, please, Gretchen?"

Gretchen looked at Christina suspiciously to see if it was a trap.

The clock clicked again, with a little quiver of the long black hand.

The passing bell rang. But neither Gretch nor anybody else fled. It was Mrs. Shevvington's class. The hallways filled with shouting and noise.

Mrs. Shevvington said at last, "Class dismissed."

I had the last word, thought Christina, her grin of delight tucked safely inside her face.

Jonah was the first to stand. He walked straight to Christina's desk. He looked down at Christina with a curiously gentle expression. He touched her hair with his fingers spread, as if resting one finger on each color hair. "You know, Chrissie," he said, a grin crossing his face, "I'm kind of attracted to you."

"Kind of!" teased the other boys.

Jonah's grin filled his face, along with his new braces, and all of him seemed to shine and laugh.

Mrs. Shevvington became nothing — merely a toad behind a desk. The entire room belonged to Jonah, and all the faces of all the seventh graders were upon him and upon Christina.

"I'm sorry I've been such a creep since that fire thing," said Jonah, loud enough for everybody to hear. "Come on, let's get out of here."

In May Christina would be fourteen. It seemed very significant. Thirteen was too young to be in love. Thirteen was playing games, imitating high school kids.

But fourteen: fourteen would be just right.

Behind Christina's house on the island grew apples. They were called Northern Spy. She loved that name.

I am the Northern Spy, thought Christina.

One advantage to old houses was that each door had a big old keyhole. Mr. Shevvington was in his study, which had a traditional mice-talking-to-Cinderella-shaped keyhole.

Christina, the Northern Spy, put her eye to the hole.

"Come in, Christina," said Mr. Shevvington. He was laughing at her. "What did you want, my dear?" he said. He waved her toward the high wooden seat in front of the desk. It was the kind of seat you could not get comfortable in. The back cut into your back, the bottom made ridges in your bottom. She remained standing.

On his desk was a stack of ordinary manila file folders. The top one was open. Stapled to the right side were papers, and to the left cover, a photograph of Dolly.

Mr. Shevvington closed Dolly's file. Then he counted the stack. Ten files: not new — wrinkled, much used.

Not future victims, thought Christina. *Past* victims. The file beneath Dolly's is Anya's, and behind that Val's. I knew there were papers! I knew it!

"How is your counseling coming along?" said Mr. Shevvington. Slowly, lovingly, he closed the briefcase. "Are you making progress?"

He knew perfectly well Christina had not said a syllable to the counselor he had picked out. And never would. "I am making a great deal of progress," said Christina. "I know the truth."

Mr. Shevvington smiled, unworried. He patted the briefcase in a friendly way, like a dog. The files were his pets. He fed them with his horrible appetites.

Neither Dolly nor Christina had homework. They played with Dolly's Barbie and Ken. Dolly had everything, from the swimsuits to the miniature hair dryer to the wedding gown. But she looked as if she would rather be reading about Barbie and Ken than dressing them. "Why aren't you reading?" said Christina. It was fun to play with Barbie and Ken. They always did what you told them to. And they always smiled and were happy to get new clothes.

"Mr. Shevvington took away my library privileges."

Christina laughed. "No, really," she said. "Why aren't you reading?"

"Mr. Shevvington says I'm not living in the real world," explained Dolly. "He says when you live entirely through characters in books it's a sign of dementia. He says I'll do demented things like — well — like — " Dolly had the grace to blush; obviously Mr. Shevvington had said she might burn clothes like Christina or go crazy like Anya. "Anyway, I'm not supposed to read every single minute."

Dolly looped her braids around her throat, chewed the tips for a while, and put high heels on Barbie. "I slipped going down Breakneck Hill, Chrissie. And yesterday I fell on the stairs. Every time I see a slant, I feel as if I'm falling. I was telling Anya and she said she always feels that way. She's felt that way since she moved here."

Christina held tighter to Ken and Barbie.

No! I'm not ready! I'm trying to survive without people to sit with at lunch. I'm trying to get through each day knowing my parents think I'm half crazy. I can't save Dolly now. I haven't saved myself. How can you be somebody else's savior when you can't be your own?

"Sometimes I think it's named for me, Chrissie."

"What is?" Christina decided to set up the barbecue for Ken to broil steaks.

"Breakneck Hill. I think I'm the one who's going to break her neck."

"No, you're not. It was named a hundred years ago for some little boy who rode his bike down it."

Christina stood Ken by the barbecue. If I don't think about what Dolly's saying, it won't be true, thought Christina.

Dolly folded her Barbie so that Barbie reclined in the bubble bath, her white toes poking up out of the tub. "Mrs. Shevvington told me that sometimes things repeat themselves when it's exactly a hundred years."

A tiny gold-and-red foil fire glinted in Ken's barbecue.

Christina thought of falls and fires. *Was it just one step from burning a person's clothes to burning that person?*

"Dolly, don't worry. You won't fall. I promise. I'll be there for you."

Dolly beamed. "And will you do another little favor for me, too, Chrissie?" A voice half whine, half love. "Would you get books for me out of your school library? I have a list. I can't get them from the elementary school library."

"Why not? Are they sex manuals?"

"Of course not. They're just stories. I can't get through the week without some good books to read."

"You mean you've read every single good book in the elementary school library?"

An odd, sly look came over Dolly's face. "Yes," she said. "That's it."

So the following day, Christina checked out five books from Dolly's list and brought them home. It was near supper. Everybody was there. Mr. and

Mrs. Shevvington, Michael, and Benj. You could not count Anya anymore. She seemed to occupy no space. Hardly more than air.

"Here are your books, Dolly," Christina said. "Hope these are good enough. The librarian had to substitute one."

Everybody stared at Christina.

"Christina," said Mr. Shevvington, "I don't know how much farther this can go. You know perfectly well we are trying to wean Dolly from her obsession with fictional characters. You know we are struggling to get her to dance and have friends over to play, instead of curling up with escape stories. And here you are, undermining our decisions, boldly and blatantly marching in here with the forbidden objects."

Christina said, "Since when do high school principals and English teachers forbid a kid to read books?"

Michael whirled on Christina. "Since they have gotten concerned for her *health*, Christina. You think we want Dolly to be some nut case like you or Anya?"

But I'm the good guy! Christina thought.

"She was always spoiled," Michael said. "The Shevvingtons are good for her. If you'd ever follow their rules, they'd be good for you, too."

What did Michael see, upstairs at night? Did he see happy, funny Dolly? Did he not notice that Dolly was afraid of more and more things every day? Did he not think that when his little sister was even afraid of frost on the windows there was something radically wrong? "She's your sister!" cried Christina. "Put her first."

Michael said very quietly, "Do you ever put me first? How many of my games have you come to since the season started, Chrissie? You and I used to be really good friends. Do you even know whether I'm a starter or whether I warm the bench? Do you know how many points I'm averaging each game? Do you know who we're playing next Friday? Have you ever brought my own sister to see me play?"

Christina flinched. While I was busy trying to be a savior, she thought, Michael stepped out of my mind like a stranger out of a bus.

"On the cupola of Schooner Inne," said Mr. Shevvington, the Perfect Principal, "is a weathervane. A copper fish. Frozen in place. No matter how the wind blows, he points the same way." Mr. Shevvington looked sadly at Christina. "No matter how the wind blows, Christina, you point only at Mrs. Shevvington and me. It's time to melt, Christina."

Michael and Benjamin and Dolly Jaye nodded.

Anya floated, unhearing.

Dolly slipped into a chair. She was small enough that her feet did not touch the floor, and she swung them a little, like a toddler.

There was ice in Christina's heart, put there by the betrayals of her parents and friends. If she melted that ice, people would be her friends again. But if she ceased to fight the Shevvingtons, nobody would fight them. They would win forever and ever, whether they wanted to humiliate Katy in English or push Dolly off the balcony.

"We're trying to help Dolly grow up," explained Benj.

Christina abandoned melting. "Why does growing up in this household always mean you can't do the things you like to do?" said Christina. "Dolly likes to read, so why can't she read?"

"I suppose the corollary to that," said Mrs. Shevvington, "is you like to burn your clothing, so why can't you burn your clothing?"

Christina hurled all five of the library books straight at Mrs. Shevvington. None of them missed.

Chapter 15

And so Christina lost her Saturday privileges again. While the others went out, she was forced to stay inside. It snowed all day: a light, friendly snow, the kind you turned your face up into and held out your tongue to collect a flake from the sky.

Mr. Shevvington went to the school, where he said he would be all day. He took his briefcase, waving it at Christina as he got into his car.

Mrs. Shevvington went to get groceries. Dolly went with her. Dolly said she loved doing errands.

How strange, thought Christina. Why doesn't Dolly go out with her friends in the sixth grade?

Dolly has no friends.

She had not asked a single sixth-grade girl over to the Inne. Nor telephoned one. Nor talked about one. She was alone every day when she met Christina after school.

Am I Dolly's only friend? thought Christina.

It was frightening. Christina's dream of coming to the mainland had been to have rafts of friends —

crowds — rooms full. At times she did. At this time she did not. But Dolly had never even used the word "friend."

Christina sat alone in the house. Even Anya was gone, working at the laundromat.

Outside the tide fumbled in Candle Cove, whispering *Ffffffff*, *Ffffffff*, *Ffffffff*. It sounded like a giant blowing out candles on a birthday cake. In a moment the whispering would turn slushy, as the rising water crawled forward, gathered momentum, and then began slamming against the rocks like trapped thunder.

No sun glinted through the mansion's windows. The color of the air was gray. The white banisters of the stairwell curled above her, like twirling cake candles. Christina climbed the stairs. She did not want to be near the cellar door.

Ffffffffff, said the cove.

At the second floor she paused.

The door to the last guest room — number eight — was open.

It seemed to Christina that she heard someone laughing.

Ffffffff, said the cove.

Christina slid into room number eight, back against the wall, in case the giggle or the tide began to rise up in the house as well.

She had never noticed before that Room 8 had a definite personality. The pencil-thin posters of the high antique bed lent a fragile air to a room decorated in lace. The colors of the room were pale, the color of ghosts. And the surprise of the room was a thick black rug with silver and gray streaks, like a storm cloud on the floor.

The colors of Anya.

Ten file folders, thought Christina Romney. Mr. Shevvington counted out ten file folders and tucked them into his briefcase.

The last two aren't yet closed — me and Dolly. Because we aren't destroyed yet. That means eight folders of girls they *have* destroyed.

Eight guest rooms.

Val, Robbie's older sister, must be the folder beneath Anya. Folder Seven. Room Seven. Slowly, as one opening a casket at a funeral home, Christina entered the room with 7 on the door.

She had been in these rooms several times. They were all different, but never before had she noticed *how* different.

Here the carpet was blue as the sea in summer, and the walls a rich violet, like sunset. The curtains were deeper blue, like night at sea. The room was small, but the dark colors did not close it in: they opened it, like a flower in a crystal vase.

It was a rich, sensuous room.

Val, sister of Robbie, on your narrow cot in your hospital room. Is this you? Are you a girl of violet and blue?

The room was as clean as a sanctuary. Waiting for its guest. But Val would never visit this room. She was trapped in another.

Christina backed out of Val's room and crossed to Number 6. She peeked in from the hall, as if Number 6 would resent being trespassed upon.

Number 6 liked yellow. Number 6 was sunshine and gold, glinting like sunrise on glass. Number 6 would love dancing and music and laughter.

Christina did not want to see Number 1, or the personalities of Numbers 2, or 3, or 4, or 5.

But she thought about Number 6 all day.

Where are you, Number 6? From what high school did they take you? Into what laundromat or what institution did they put you?

Several days later, over supper, Michael talked relentlessly about basketball. The team was sixteen and nine, and if they won tonight's game, they would go into the regional play-offs. He said almost shyly to Christina, "It was nice to see you at practice this afternoon."

"You were terrific," she said to him. "Especially at suicide."

Michael grinned. "I love suicide."

"You *what*?" said Dolly.

"Suicide," explained Christina, "is when the coach makes the boys run full speed into the wall, slam into it, pivot around, race back across the gym, slam into that wall, pivot, race back across the gym, slam into — "

"I get the point," said Dolly. "And this is what my brother is good at? Why don't they give it a peaceful name, like, say, Double Wall Approach?"

"Because it's not peaceful," said Benjamin. "It's supposed to turn the team into warriors. Make them want to stomp the other team." Benjamin was teasing his younger brother.

"What is it you guys yell when you huddle on the edge of the court just before the game begins?" Dolly wanted to know.

Michael grinned again. "Sometimes we yell '*Defense!*' and sometimes we yell '*Team work!*' but last week we yelled '*Crunch 'em!*,' and we scored so high that we're always gonna yell '*Crunch 'em!*' from now on."

Dolly said, "I hope skiing is more civilized."

The Shevvingtons smiled.

Michael said, "I phoned Mom and Dad and got permission. But there's one little problem. I don't want to go. We're having an extra practice that weekend and I'd rather do that. So if you don't mind, Mrs. Shevvington, and thanks a lot for offering. I'll spend the weekend with George instead."

No! thought Christina. I need you. You haven't noticed anything wrong with Dolly or the Shevvingtons yet, but I need your body and your muscles and your presence over the ski weekend!

"Fine idea," said Mr. Shevvington. "George's family are fine people. I approve heartily of your dedication to the team spirit, Michael."

Michael did not notice the falseness in this silly sentence; it was the kind of remark he expected from a principal. "Gotta run. You coming to the game, Chrissie?"

"Yes," said Christina. "Dolly and I both are."

"Oh, no," said Dolly. "I have homework." Her brother stood very still. Christina had been stabbed like that many times this year. She had not known Michael was getting stabbed. "I bought tickets,

Dolly," said Christina. "You can do your homework at halftime. We need to see Michael play."

"Don't worry about it," said Michael. He was into his coat and out the door in moments.

Anya said, "I'll go to the game with you, Chrissie. May I use Dolly's ticket?"

They were so startled that Anya was still a living, speaking presence that nobody spoke. "That's great, Anya," Christina managed. "I'd love that. Finish your supper. We have to leave pretty soon."

They had plenty of time actually, but to get Anya ready to appear in public might take half an evening.

Dolly asked Mrs. Shevvington if they could do her homework together. "It's more fun that way," she said, smiling up at Mrs. Shevvington.

Benjamin said, "Listen. If Michael's not going skiing, I don't want to. At the gas station they'll pay me overtime. How about I stay at George's, too? They have lots of room."

Benj's expression did not change like his brother's or sister's. There was no excitement, pleading, or enthusiasm. It was stolid. A fisherman's face. He waited patiently for the Shevvingtons' decision.

It came as no surprise to Christina that Mr. Shevvington felt this was a Fine Idea. Dedication to a Personal Goal. It was What Growing Up Was All About. Benj grunted and left the table.

So it would be Dolly, Anya, and Christina going skiing. *Anya can't even comb her hair, and Dolly wants to be crunched.*

She would probably begin giggling with hysteria when they reached the ski resort, get locked up like

Val or Number 6, leaving the Shevvingtons free to manipulate Dolly's fear of heights on the Killer Slopes.

There was, Christina remembered, a ski trail called Suicide.

Perhaps they would start Dolly out on that one.

Anya came running down the stairs. "Are we going?" she said anxiously to Christina. Christina could remember when Anya wore a dark navy blue coat set off by a crimson scarf and soft, supple gloves with a purse that matched. Now Anya had gotten into an old ski jacket whose down was leaking out the seams. She'd rammed a ragged ski cap over her hair without checking in the mirror. One ear showed, the other didn't.

Christina wanted to shake her by the shoulders. *Why can't you pull yourself together? Why do you have to keep rowing with one oar?*

But she loved Anya. "Here," she said quietly. "Let me button your coat for you." Anya had started with the first button, but the second hole. Christina fixed her and walked her to the front door.

Anya took her hand when they reached the sidewalk. "Slippery," she confided.

You don't know how slippery, thought Christina.

The two girls hiked.

If Blake were here, he'd drive us in his beautiful red sports car, thought Christina. She wondered if Anya had finished that letter to Blake and put a stamp on it and dropped it off at the post office. It seemed far more than Anya was capable of. Anyway, she hadn't asked Blake for help. Only told him they were having tea and toast.

By now Blake surely had a new girlfriend to match himself: beautiful and well dressed and sleek. Why would he bother again with Anya?

Anya said, "Chrissie, I can't wait to go skiing."

Christina was amazed. Anya was being brought on the ski trip rather like a suitcase or a bathrobe. Nobody expected her to ski. "That's great, Anya," said Christina. "Do you know how to ski?"

"No," said Anya. She laughed — a real laugh — her old laugh. "But Blake does."

Christina repeated, "Blake?"

Anya's joyous laugh rang like church bells. "Blake answered my letter," she said. "His boarding school is only a few miles away from the ski resort we're going to. He's meeting me!"

Christina gasped. Blake — an ally! Right there! Blake had known more about the Shevvingtons than anybody, and Blake had believed. "Anya, you didn't tell the Shevvingtons about this, did you? They don't know, do they?"

"Tell the Shevvingtons?" said Anya. "What — do you think I'm crazy?"

They both laughed. Gales of sane girlish laughter.

At last, at last — they knew something the Shevvingtons didn't.

Chapter 16

"Don't tell Dolly," whispered Christina.

Anya nodded. "I won't. Dolly loves the Shevvingtons."

"But how did you get a letter back from Blake? The Shevvingtons get all the mail first."

"I put the laundromat as my return address," said Anya. Her huge, dark eyes flickered in her chalk-white face, like a poster child from a country filled with starvation. "I don't have any clothes to wear, Chrissie. I've never been skiing."

"Neither have I. The Shevvingtons bought Dolly a beautiful emerald-green ski suit. She looks like a Christmas tree ornament."

"I know. I saw. You and I will have to come up with something. I have to look perfect for Blake."

Christina thought this was the most romantic thing ever to happen. True love was going to rescue Anya.

We'll whip the Shevvingtons! she thought. Blake and Anya and I.

Now Christina could hardly wait for the three-day weekend.

The joy of revenge bubbled in Christina like soda pop. When she and Anya entered the high school, she was all but dancing. They handed their cardboard tickets to the kid at the gym door and got their hands stamped with the school initials. Biting their lips to contain their wild laughter, they took two steps — and Mr. Shevvington blocked the way.

She had forgotten that the principal attended home games.

"Anya," he said. His voice was soft. He wet his lips. "You look so lively. Has something happened?"

Anya put up quivering hands to protect herself from the piercing shaft of his eyes. They were blue tonight, blank as insanity.

Mr. Shevvington took Anya's wrists and lowered her hands. "Tell me, Anya," he coaxed.

She would tell. Christina knew it. Then the Shevvingtons would know, could protect themselves, and what was worse, would laugh at Christina for deluding herself that she could beat them.

"I decided to kick butt, Mr. Shevvington," Christina said crudely. "I'm gonna shape her up. I put lots of makeup on her. She's gonna scream for the team or else."

Legs flaring left, pompons rustling right, the cheerleaders were shouting, *"Michael, Michael, he's our man, if he can't do it, no one can!"*

"Christina, Christina, she's our man," said Christina to the principal. "If she can't do it, no one can."

Mr. Shevvington laughed. "Getting her cheeks

rosy with rouge, Christina, is hardly putting her back together again."

Anya said fretfully, "It's noisy in here, Crissie. I wanna go home."

"I'll be with you," said Christina. "Don't whimper."

Anya dipped further into baby talk. "I'na go home," she mumbled.

Mr. Shevvington smiled and turned away to greet a basketball parent.

"Oh, Arthur," said the parent adoringly. "You're not only here for every game, you don't miss the Junior Varsity either. It gives the boys such a boost that their principal always supports them. With your schedule I just don't know how you do it."

Christina yanked Anya by her coat collar. On the bleachers the kids were kicking the boards with their heels. "Air ball, air ball, air ball!" screamed the kids hopefully.

At games the kids bunched by grade, and within that bunch by cliques. Christina had never been to a game before and did not know where to sit. Anya no longer had a grade or a clique. There's Jennie, Christina thought with relief, and behind her is Robbie.

Christina hauled Anya over coats, between couples, and up four rows. Anya continued whimpering and resisting. Christina could not tell if Anya was acting for Mr. Shevvington's sake or if she had slipped back into her old self. She could hardly ask. ("Are you sane or not right now, Anya?") Christina found a space big enough for two and shoved Anya down. She sat — and found Gretchen and Vicki on her right.

"What're you doing here?" said Gretch.

"We came to see Michael."

"It's about time," said Vicki.

They watched the game. Two minutes by the time clock, eight minutes in real life.

Gretch said critically, "Anya looks pretty decent. She must be getting someplace with her psychiatrist."

Anya's cheeks stained red. Christina considered snapping off Gretchen's fingers, when she realized it was the first time in months that Anya had been sufficiently aware to be hurt. Christina squeezed Anya's hand for comfort, and Anya squeezed back. She's in there! thought Christina, and her joy soared to the gym ceiling.

"So are you going skiing on the three-day weekend?" said Gretchen to Christina. "We always go. We have our own condo, of course. And season passes, so we don't have to wait in line the way you'll have to. What kind of boots do you have? Mine're new this year, of course."

Christina had nothing.

Gretch said, "You've never seen my new ski outfit either, Christina. It's the height of fashion. I'm a very good skier, of course. Which slope will you be on? The bunny slope?" She giggled. "Last weekend when we were skiing, two kids broke their legs right there on the bunny slope. We laughed so hard."

You are pond scum, thought Christina. Sewer sludge.

Vicki leaned over. "I suppose you'll have blue jeans on. The first time you fall you'll be soaked."

"That'll be in sixty seconds," said Gretch.

Vicki and Gretch laughed and laughed.

Anya flushed.

Christina had seen the outfit Gretchen had ordered. She had shown it to the whole seventh grade. Gleaming synthetic skiwear that clung to the body like colored water. The kind of clothing perfect people wore.

Christina thought, Blake will be a fine skier. He's that kind of person. He won't want an Anya who falls over and is clumsy and wearing wet jeans. He'll want somebody beautiful and graceful and brilliant.

What if Anya did not measure up? What if Blake abandoned them?

Christina shut it out of her mind. She watched Michael play. He was very good. Not enough height, but he made up for it in speed.

I don't have enough height, either, thought Christina. But I am going to make up for it in cleverness. So there.

The next morning the Shevvingtons said they were signing Dolly up for Beginner Ski Class. "You'll have such fun, Dolly, darling," they said. "It's children your age, with a very understanding, gentle instructor. Before you know it, you'll be a pro!"

Christina could not help herself. "A class?" she said eagerly. "I don't know how to ski either. May I take the class, too? I don't mind being in with little kids."

Mrs. Shevvington raised her caterpillar eyebrows above her bran-muffin face. "Really, Christina," she said. "I hardly think your recent behavior warrants such a reward." She turned back to Dolly. "And guess what else I got for you," she said.

Again Christina could not help herself. She looked to Anya for comfort. Anya rolled her eyes and pantomimed.

What if the Shevvingtons saw? What if the Shevvingtons found out that Anya was healing? What might Mr. Shevvington do to get her soul back?

Dolly said, "I don't care. I don't want to ski. I don't want to go downhill anywhere, ever."

Christina studied her breakfast cereal to keep herself from looking in Anya's direction. She must never look at Anya again. It would betray them both.

"You won't break any bones," said Mr. Shevvington. "You're so light and graceful, Dolly, you'll land like a baby bird."

"I won't! I'll land on my face. I can feel it. I dream about it. The ice will rip my face and tear my hair. Please don't make me! Give the class to Chrissie. She wants it. I'll just sit in the ski lodge and read a book by the fire. Please don't make me go!" Dolly put her hands over her face, not to weep behind her fingers, but to save herself from landing face first.

"Dolly, see the lovely gloves I bought you?" said Mrs. Shevvington. "And you won't fall. You'll have poles to keep you up. All those dancing lessons will stand you in good stead now."

Dolly took the gloves.

Christina had never seen such gloves. A green so dark and shimmering it was like the sea underwater, fabric so supple it was like skin — yet thick and waterproof.

The mittens her mother knitted seemed made for a heavy, ugly farm wife.

I want gloves like that, thought Christina.

She wanted to take them from Dolly's hands and put them on her own hands, and —

Jealousy was alive in her, snatching her good thoughts to make them bad. The Shevvingtons were smiling. The gloves aren't for Dolly, Christina thought. They're for me. To bring out the worst in me. To make me abandon Dolly.

At lunch in the cafeteria she told Jonah everything. He listened with his whole body. His sandwich hung untouched in his hand; he ate her words instead. "It's looking good," said Jonah. "Blake's a great guy. With him there they can't do much."

"They did before. They convinced Blake's parents to ship him off to boarding school, and Blake couldn't fight back. All of a sudden he was gone."

"They can't manage that in a weekend," Jonah pointed out. "Blake will protect Anya just fine." Jonah frowned slightly. He took a huge bite out of his sandwich. Through layers of ham and cheese, he said, "Blake always liked you. And you always liked him."

"I think he's terrific. That's why I feel so good about this weekend."

Jonah took a more savage bite. "He's old," he said contemptuously. "He's got to be eighteen."

Jonah was jealous. Christina, ignoring several hundred witnesses, leaned across the cafeteria table and kissed Jonah on the mouth.

He couldn't kiss back — he was eating. His eyes flew open with amazement, and he struggled with his ham and cheese. By the time he finished chewing, half the seventh grade had begun a football cheer — *"First in ten, do it again!"*

They gathered around Christina and Jonah, saying, "Well? Going to return the favor, Jonah? Come on. Let's see your technique."

Jonah threw his lunch bag at them but paper bags are poor weapons, and nothing happened, so he threw his orange.

Kenny threw back an apple. Jonah threw his half-empty chocolate milk. Ellen hurled her pudding, and within moments they were having the food fight of the year. People were taking advantage of this wonderful moment to even scores with people they had detested. Hot lunch people, who had spaghetti, emptied spaghetti down each other's sweaters. Christina found a plate, its tomato sauce untouched in a puddle on the white pasta, and considered Gretchen's white cashmere sweater.

"Who started this?" shouted the cafeteria proctor, racing among the tables.

"Christina did," said Gretchen.

Christina stood very still, the spaghetti plate balanced on her palm as if she were a waitress serving dinners.

The proctor said grimly. "Well, Miss Romney, Mr. Shevvington will not be surprised to have you brought to his office yet again."

Christina set down the spaghetti.

She had unknowingly played right into Mr. Shevvington's hands.

He would take away the ski weekend.

Dolly and Anya would go without her.

Chapter 17

"Mr. Shevvington is not in the office at the moment," said the secretary, barely glancing up. It was what secretaries did best at this school — ignore the students. "He's showing the school board members the leaking roof in the west wing. You'll have to wait."

Christina sat quietly on a bench in the outer office. One secretary typed, one filed, one talked on the phone, and one scrolled down a computer screen. The clerk who was typing finished. "I'm going to take this down to the science department," she said. The one filing said, "I'm going on break now," and waltzed out. The clerk on the phone argued with her caller, glaring into the receiver. The computer operator moaned, pressing her hands over her eyes. "Oh, no, I did this wrong; I have to do it over."

Christina glided without sound across the office. She turned the handle to Mr. Shevvington's office, opened the door, and crept in.

The briefcase, bulging, sat under Mr. Shevvington's desk.

I have it! she exulted. I knew eventually I would win. Good *does* triumph over evil.

She wrapped her fingers around the handle. She walked past the clerk with computer problems and the clerk with telephone problems. Neither paid any attention. She walked out of the office.

She had taken two steps toward her locker when Mr. Shevvington appeared way down the hall, coming toward her. He was with a man and woman: the school board members.

Christina walked the other way. She did not run. Running made people realize there was something wrong. She knew she was recognized. Only Christina had the hair of three colors. And no student, even the most geeky nerds, carried a briefcase. But Mr. Shevvington had his image to keep up. He was not going to shout, "Stop thief!" in front of school board members. Besides, she might show them the contents.

Christina walked quickly the opposite way. It was a high school wing; the junior high students were not normally in the same halls as high school kids. The school had many wings radiating outward for the junior and senior high, with gymnasiums, auditorium, music rooms, and art department in the middle.

"Please excuse me," said Mr. Shevvington in a leisurely voice. "I have a discipline problem to attend to. I will telephone you after I have the figures on what it will cost to repair the roof."

Christina reached the end of her corridor. She could turn left or right. And once out of Mr. Shevvington's sight, she could run.

Any exit, she thought. Leave school. Run through town. Go to the harbor. I'll hide the briefcase on somebody's boat. If Frankie is there I'll talk him into taking me back to the island right now.

Her mind raced over hiding places, escape routes, dark corners.

"Always a pleasure to deal with you, Arthur," boomed the school board member.

She wanted to look back and see if they were shaking hands or if he was already headed her way. She made herself keep going. She turned right. Shifting the heavy briefcase to her other hand, Christina began to run.

A high school teacher lecturing in his doorway stepped backward into the hall and frowned. She smiled back. "You have a pass?" he demanded.

Christina hoisted the briefcase instead of a pass. "Mr. Shevvington asked me to bring him his briefcase," she said, slowing her pace. The teacher nodded, watching her as she walked on. Now she could not run anymore. Heart pounding like a sprinter's, she kept her steps slow. The corridor was horribly long. She was two thirds of the way down, approaching the next crossing of corridors, when Mr. Shevvington turned the corner behind her. "Christina," he called after her.

She continued walking.

"Christina," he said again.

She reached the next turning. Each hall had an

EXIT sign at the far end. But where did they come out? The hall had no windows for her to figure it out. What if she came out in the teachers' parking lot, where walls enclosed the cars, and she had to run around the entire building? What if she came out the rear and had to cross the open playing fields like a rabbit in front of a shotgun?

Passing bells rang.

High school students spurted out of their classrooms. Screaming, shoving, laughing, shouting, they filled the hall like a volcano erupting. She turned right.

Boys who stood a foot higher than Christina, girls whose sweaters swirled like choir robes, academic types with books stacked like chimney bricks, surrounded her. She hugged the briefcase to her and slipped through, dodging and curving.

Taking advantage of a swarm of enormous football-shouldered boys, Christina ducked into a stairwell and ran up the stairs.

Mr. Shevvington's voice rang in the shaft below. "Did you boys see a little seventh-grade girl? Strange multi-colored hair?"

"The little island girl," said one agreeably. "Anya's little friend." This speaker must have pointed, because Mr. Shevvington said, "Thanks," and his feet pounded on the stairs like pistons.

She flung open the door and emerged on the second floor.

Terrible place to be. If only she could dump the briefcase somewhere.

How barren the school seemed, now that she

needed a hiding place. Hallways of gleaming tile and no furniture. Doors opening into classrooms filled by waiting teachers. Every closet locked by janitors, every office staffed.

"Christina! Christina Romney!" Mr. Shevvington was shouting now. It was too late to be subtle. He was afraid. The briefcase mattered. She had to win!

But now she was in the junior high wing, where everybody knew her name. Where some teacher was sure to grab her and hold her prisoner. In seconds passing period would be over. The halls would be empty. She would be exposed.

"Christina!"

She was panicking. The hand gripping the briefcase cramped and ached. Seventh-grade faces caught hers, staring, surprised, confused. Christina rushed on. Mr. Shevvington strode after her.

She reached the other stairwell and yanked open the door. Down she ran. Behind her the bells rang; passing period was over; when she got to the bottom and came out again in front of the office where she had begun, she would be the only child in sight. Carrying the only briefcase in sight.

The tears began. How she hated Mr. Shevvington for having the power to make her cry! How she hated herself for being only thirteen and weak!

Halfway down the stairs she ran straight into Gretchen.

How could it be that Christina had prayed for assistance — and it was Gretchen who appeared! She whispered, "Gretchen, please help me. Take this briefcase. Hide it in your locker. Don't tell anybody. It's a matter of life and death."

Gretchen stared at her. Christina thrust the briefcase into her hands. "Run, Gretchen! Please!"

"But Christina, this is Mr. Shevvington's. I recognize it. He carries it everywhere he goes. What are you doing with it?"

"I stole it. It has papers I have to have."

Gretchen gasped.

They both heard the heavy pounding of feet. Mr. Shevvington running. She might not accomplish anything else, but she had made him desperate.

Gretchen took the briefcase and fled.

Mr. Shevvington yanked open the stairwell door. Christina watched his shadow. He looked up to see if she had tried to get out on the roof. He looked down to see if she had returned to the first floor. Christina caught the door behind Gretchen and let it close without a sound.

Mr. Shevvington raced down the stairs.

"You scared me, Mr. Shevvington," she said calmly. "Chasing me like that."

He stopped two steps above her, trying to see the briefcase. Alone in the stairwell they faced each other. How tall he was, with those two extra steps for height!

He put his hands forward, as if to shake her until her spine snapped. Christina jumped away, ripped open the door, and came out in front of the two school board members, still talking. She pretended her shoelace was undone, and knelt to tie it up again.

"Why, Arthur," said one pleasantly, "that was

quick. You're always so efficient. We had another thought about how to solve the roof problem. Do you have a minute?"

Christina double knotted it. She untied and tied the other shoe.

"Of course," said Mr. Shevvington smoothly. "Come into my office."

Christina was alone in the hall. Unsteadily she got to her feet. Where was Gretchen's locker? She tottered toward the junior high lockers.

She heaved an enormous sigh of relief, and the extra oxygen calmed her. I'll take the briefcase. I'll skip the rest of school. I'll —

Gretchen popped out of the girls' bathroom. "You're safe, Christina," she said. "I owe you for being nice to me in class. So I will never tell anybody you stole Mr. Shevvington's briefcase. I snuck into his office and put it under his desk. Those dumb secretaries didn't even look up. I even locked the door after me. Mr. Shevvington can't accuse you of taking it now. It looks like it was there all along."

Christina stood very still.

"Are you all right?" whispered Gretchen nervously.

He was in his office right now with the school board. When he sat down, his polished shoes would hit the briefcase. He would have the last laugh.

He will always have the last laugh, thought Christina.

I am no longer sure that good triumphs over evil.

I am afraid that evil will win.

Chapter 18

After school the children all gathered around Christina. "What was your punishment?" they said. "What did he do to you?" The food fight was ancient history. She had almost forgotten it.

My punishment, she thought, is knowing that he has won and will always win. Knowing that someday an empty room in an empty inn will be decorated with my personality. "Nothing. Just gave me a hard time."

Jonah marvelled. "You must have a silver tongue, Chrissie," he said.

Mr. Shevvington had thought she put the briefcase under his desk herself, from fear of him. He couldn't figure out how she had done it, but he had excused the food fight because the briefcase was such a joke.

"Everybody come to my house," Jonah called. "I turned on the outside water faucet and sprayed the snow maze with the hose. It iced up. We can slide on it!"

Half the seventh grade wanted to go to Jonah's.

Christina said she was coming but she had to wait for Dolly. The children ran on.

Dolly appeared almost immediately. Christina extended her hand, but Dolly didn't take it. "I've outgrown holding hands," said Dolly. "Mrs. Shevvington says I must learn to stand alone."

Christina knew that none of them could stand alone against the Shevvingtons. "How awful!" said Christina. "Dolly, sometimes you need to hold hands."

Dolly was blue from cold. She looked, in the island phrase, peak-ed. Christina told her about Jonah's ice maze and how they would all slip and slide together. Dolly was not enthusiastic.

Jonah's mother gave everybody old holey socks to slip over their shoes. About twenty seventh-graders — kids Christina most and least liked: Robbie, Katy, Gretch — slithered through the ice mazes on socky feet. They collided at intersections, made trains of themselves, and pushed each other into dead ends.

Dolly refused to go into the maze. "I might get lost," she said seriously.

The seventh-graders howled with laughter. "It's just my backyard," said Jonah nicely. "And the maze isn't very deep, Dolly. If you stand up straight, it's waist high. Nothing can happen to you."

"It looks like Breakneck Hill Road," said Dolly. "All ice and downhill."

The seventh-graders ignored Dolly and chased

each other, slipping, sliding, and shrieking in the maze.

Kenny had a long stadium scarf, knitted in purple-and-white squares. Everybody hung onto it, and Kenny dragged them after him.

Dolly went inside to have hot chocolate with Jonah's mother. Mrs. Bergeron said, "Christina, honey? I wonder if you'd come in, too, for a moment. I have something to show you."

Christina was suspicious of adults with something to show her. She went in uneasily, keeping her back to the wall.

Outside, Jonah led an ice war.

Mrs. Bergeron poured a mug of hot chocolate for Dolly and dropped five tiny marshmallows into it. Dolly stirred happily, watching them melt.

Mrs. Bergeron put a large white cardboard box on the table. Tissue poked out of the sides. "Ooooh, clothes," said Dolly. "I love clothes. Did you buy something new, Mrs. Bergeron?"

"Yes, but this is the old one. I wore it only once, and it just wasn't me. It made me feel sallow and fat." She took off the lid. Color as bright as lemons sang from the box.

Mrs. Bergeron unfolded a ski jacket so beautiful, so sunny-yellow and snowy-white that the little girls blinked. She held it up against Christina. "It's a tiny bit large," she admitted. "But that doesn't matter when you're skiing." She unfolded the ski pants. "A tiny bit long," she said. "But when you ski, you need that extra room for flexibility."

Christina trembled.

Mrs. Bergeron said, "Let's just slip it on. Make sure it's right for you, Christina. I will feel so much better if this ski suit gets some use."

Christina put it on. She said nothing. Her heart was too full for speech.

Dolly whispered, "Ooooh, Chrissie. Your hair glitters. It's like you're wearing new-fallen snow."

Mrs. Bergeron led her upstairs to a full-length mirror, and Christina stared at herself, a daffodil in the snow.

"I look perfect in mine, too," said Dolly. "Mine's emerald green. It's just right for my hair, too. My hair is red," she added, as if Mrs. Bergeron could not see.

Mrs. Bergeron said, "Everything is easier to handle when you're dressed just right and your hair is perfect."

Christina wanted to hug Mrs. Bergeron and to be hugged: have her anxiety hugged away as this ski suit would take away the grief of having to wear old blue jeans. But she was too weary with fears to raise her arms.

Mrs. Bergeron hugged her anyway.

Mothers — the most wonderful people in the world. Christina pretended Mrs. Bergeron was her own mother. She sank into the hug. Jonah's mother said, "When you reach the ski resort, why, you'll slip into this and be the most beautiful girl on the slopes." Folding the lemony snow puffs of jacket and pants, she tucked them into a dark brown shopping bag. It was hidden in there, a secret victory for Christina.

"Thank you," Christina whispered.

Mrs. Bergeron said, "Nonsense. Now you two go out there and get some fresh air. You need a little color in your cheeks."

Outside the snowball battles had reached war proportions. Teams were spread across the yards with snipers in trees, while officers built caches of snowballs to supply their soldiers with.

Christina ran to find Jonah. "You told your mother I didn't have a ski suit," she said.

"Are you mad?"

"No! It's so beautiful!"

Jonah looked at her with that new intense heat that had shocked her before. But neither could act on it. They were pelted with snowballs as the opposite team caught them unaware.

The sun sank in the sky: ripples of pink and purple flung like ribbons into the snow-threatening distance. The children were incredibly beautiful against the snow. Scarlet, blue, green, and gold were their jackets and scarves. Like a medieval pageant, they trooped on a white world.

And Christina, when it was time to go home, held in a brown paper bag her second secret: clothes that would give her the strength to ski.

Chapter 19

The girls shared a bedroom. It had one bunk bed and one double bed on each side of an enormous diamond-shaped window that looked right out on the ski slopes. The bare wood floor was slippery and smelled of wax. On the bathroom door was a mirror panel, in front of which Dolly preened. She was a pixie. Anya had French-braided the gleaming red hair in a single tight row from her forehead back to the nape of her neck: Dolly's lovely little head, slender neck, and tiny wrists were all that showed beneath the emerald green wrapper of ski suit. Dolly turned left and turned right, looked back over her shoulder and dipped.

"You're perfect," said Mrs. Shevvington, entering the room.

Dolly looked up shyly, as eager for Mrs. Shevvington's compliments as Christina would have been for Blake's. Dolly said, "I'm still afraid of falling." She shivered, looking fragile as glass.

Mrs. Shevvington was already shaped like a refrigerator. In her padded ski suit she looked like a wicked, beardless Santa Claus. Next to her, Dolly was a miniature person, a pet, like a miniature poodle. Mrs. Shevvington patted Dolly like a dog, too.

Christina was undressed, but she had not taken the yellow ski suit out of its brown paper bag. The jeans she had peeled off lay in a messy inside-out pile on the floor. Anya had nothing to change into. The pitiful old ski jacket with its stains and tears hung loosely on her narrow shoulders.

Mrs. Shevvington's eyes passed over Christina and Anya, and she was satisfied with what she saw. To Dolly she said, "Of course you'll fall. Beginners always fall. But it's just tipping over, and slithering on the snow for a few feet. The bunny slope is made for falling. And before you know it, you'll be sailing down Gentle Deer, which is the advanced-beginner trail and then Running Deer, which is intermediate."

Into Christina's ear, Anya breathed, "What if he doesn't come?" Her beauty was like a thread — anything could cut it through. He will, promised Christina soundlessly.

Dolly took Mrs. Shevvington's hand. "Are you sure I won't fall very hard?"

"Even if you do, look how padded you are. A baby doesn't get hurt when it sits down because of its diapers. And you won't either."

Dolly beamed up at Mrs. Shevvington. "You always know what to say."

"We decided," Mrs. Shevvington added, "that it would be best to sign you all up for a beginner class. After all, we don't want any broken bones in the first five minutes, do we?" She smiled, her little corn teeth the only color in her oatmeal face, as if she had scheduled the broken bones for later on. "So Anya, Christina, hurry and get ready. We'll meet you at the bunny slope in a few moments."

They had to cover their tracks, of course. Adoring school parents must be able to compliment the Shevvingtons no matter what happened to Dolly.

Dolly said to Christina, "And you didn't trust the Shevvingtons to make this a perfect weekend." She hugged Mrs. Shevvington. "You knew I needed beginner company to fall with, didn't you?" she said lovingly. "Thank you for being nice to Christina even when she's difficult." Dolly and Mrs. Shevvington left the room without a backward glance.

Christina took her turn in front of the mirror. Slowly she slid her legs into the puffy, satiny folds of the ski pants. She fastened the suspenders and adjusted the high waist. Holding her turtleneck sleeves with her fingertips so they wouldn't get caught in the jacket, she put on the daffodil-yellow top. Slowly she zipped it up, watching her reflection. She ran her ten fingers into her hair and fluffed it around the collar. I'm pretty, she thought. She wondered if Blake would tell her so, if he would grin when he saw her and yell, "Hey Chrissie, I've missed you!" If he would say, "Gosh, you look pretty; yellow is your color."

Anya whispered, "Chrissie! Look out the window!"

Outdoors, the snow fell thickly and steadily in a harsh wind.

It was like seeing through a lace curtain. People were blurred and snow laden.

Like the Shevvingtons, most people on the slopes wore dark fashion colors: magenta, jade, or navy. When I am out there, Christina thought, I will blend with the weather and the mountains and the sky — lemon yellow with white. I will be beautiful. Different. Memorable.

Anya was pointing. Her thin, ringless finger was trembling.

Christina looked harder and saw Blake.

Blake! No cap, even in this cruel wind, just a scarlet headband that lifted his dark hair and protected his ears, and a high-necked scarlet jacket that snuggled under his chin. Across the ski suit was a silver metallic slash from chest to knee. He seemed taller to Christina, and he was certainly broader. He wore his ski boots and held his skis, which he was resting in the snow as he examined every person coming out the lodge doors. After a while he turned to look in other directions. The snow glittered white and furious, and he slid sunglasses onto the bridge of his nose.

He held the snow as an actor holds the stage. It was his.

People paused when they saw him, admired him for a moment, and gave him space: he was too impressive to shoulder out of the way.

Blake, I love you! Christina sent her message by heart. Then, guiltily, she turned to look at Anya, who loved him, too.

Anya's hair had worked loose. Its dark tendrils

curled around the ragged old hood. Her thin ivory face was as translucent as the sky at dawn. "He came," she breathed. Tears filled her eyes, and she rested both palms on the icy window, staring down at Blake. The wind attacked Blake and lifted his hair but he did not move, surveying the skiers, looking for Anya.

Anya looked down at herself. At the ugly maroon jacket, the wrong length for her, not quite warm enough, the rips she had not mended. Her cheeks stained red. She took a painful little breath, lifted her chin, and said, "I love him. Love doesn't need perfect clothes."

She kissed Christina. "Cancel me out of the beginner class," she whispered. "Blake will teach me."

Christina held her daydreams for another second: a wonderful instant of Blake's love, Blake's touch, Blake's company. Then she said, "Quick. Switch clothes with me. You have to look perfect for Blake."

"No," said Anya. "Mrs. Bergeron gave them to you. So Gretch- and Vicki-types wouldn't laugh at you."

"I know how to laugh back," said Christina. She was unzipped, she was unbuttoned, she was peeling it away. She was trying not to cry.

Anya bit her lips, staring not at Christina but at the lemony fluff piling by Christina's feet. Then with desperate speed she ripped off her ugly old things and yanked on the yellow. They had been too big for Christina; they were slightly too snug for Anya: but it made her slim and fragile instead of the padded pillow so many skiers resembled. Christina teased Anya's hair into tiny black curls beneath the daffodil trim.

Anya whispered, "Thank you, Chrissie," and hugged her, and ran out of the room. Christina, slowly putting back on her own jeans and her regular old winter jacket and scarves, stood by the diamond window, watching Blake.

All her life she would remember Anya coming down the steps of the lodge — how Blake half knew her and half didn't. How he suddenly flung back his head, and laughed, and tore off his sunglasses. How he strode forward, folded back the yellow hood and, with his bare hands in that terrible cold, held her face up to his. Tilted her head back, kissed her cold lips, and spoke to her and kissed her again.

Christina was a silly little seventh-grader, alone in a snow-cold world.

Blake loved Anya. Always had, always would.

The bunny slope was hardly even a bump. There was no chair lift to the top, but a rope, like a clothesline on a pulley. The class had all ages in it: nervous middle-aged women and fearless toddlers. Nobody else was wearing jeans. Dolly frowned. "I thought you said you had gotten good clothes somewhere," she said. "Were you yarning again, Chrissie? You have to stop that. It's a very bad habit."

Mr. and Mrs. Shevvington said, "Now, Dolly. Be generous. Forgive Christina her lies."

I'm the one who's generous! thought Christina, yearning for credit.

But she could not tell them; they still didn't know about Blake, and they certainly would not recognize Anya in her lemon yellow. The more time Anya had with Blake before the Shevvingtons knew, the more her strength would return.

The wind went through the denim fabric as if her legs were bare.

Skiing turned out to be like riding a bicycle: once you had it, you had it. The first time down Christina was fine; the second time she fell twice; the third time she fell once; the fourth time she was fine again. "This is fun!" she said to Dolly, and to her astonishment Dolly's little cheeks were red with joy, and Dolly nodded. "I love it!" she cried against the wind. "I think I'm going to be good at it!"

The wind lifted Christina's hair like banners of silver and gold. The instructor cried, "What beautiful hair! I've never seen hair like that. Is it real?"

Christina and Dolly laughed together.

The snow and the slopes had turned them back into friends: it was like the island: it pulled them together, it made them one.

The Shevvingtons had vanished. They were dressed in dark blue. The moment they skied away and got in line somewhere they became invisible. I will never know where they are, thought Christina Romney, and felt a chill that was not wind factor.

In only two hours they graduated. "Great work, girls," said the instructor approvingly. "Now right over there are Gentle Deer and Running Deer. Use the ski lift. I'll watch you the first time, and then you're on your own because I'll be starting another class. Don't try Running Deer yet. It's a little tricky for the first day."

"Gentle Deer," repeated Dolly. "Doesn't it sound like an Indian mother, rocking her papoose?" The two girls got in line for their first chair lift. The brutal wind had kept many people indoors. Only a dozen skiers were in front of them: several adults wearing navy. Nobody looked thick enough to be Mrs. Shevvington, nor lean and elegant enough to be Mr. Shevvington.

The ski lift had a metal seat no wider and no more substantial than a backyard swing's. The back was a wide metal bar, and in front a thin metal bar snapped in place. The wind rocked the chairs back and forth. Each time the lift stopped for the next passenger, the skiers higher up jerked. Their legs dangled above the open snow. They went higher and higher in the sky, until far up Gentle Deer they vanished in the swirling snow, eaten by the mountain.

"I can't," whimpered Dolly. "I'll fall, Chrissie. I don't want to do this, Chrissie, don't make me, Chrissie, let's go inside and get warm at the fire, Chrissie — "

An attendant plopped them backward onto the thin metal seat, swung the bar closed, and they were snatched up the mountain, two by two.

Christina was terrified. She had not known how high it would be. How flimsy. Gripping the bar in her mittens she choked back a sob of fear. When Dolly twisted around, the chair swung hideously. They both screamed. Behind them two kids about five years old called, "What are you so worried about? This is nothing. Don't make a big deal over it." Shamed, Christina and Dolly grit their teeth and prayed, teetering over the tops of the pointed firs. Every few yards the horrible little container jerked again, picking up more skiers.

At the top came the next terror — how to get off. They desperately studied the people ahead but couldn't quite see how it was done. An attendant thrust open the bar and Christina lurched out, tumbling ingloriously and falling on her bottom. Dolly vaulted off, landing perfectly and then tipping over slowly. "We're alive," whispered Dolly, lying on her side, giggling like a maniac. The five-year-olds rolled their eyes and took off immediately, sailing on the snow as easily as island children sailed on the sea.

Bodies leaning left and leaning right, poles angled for balance, scarves flying out, skiers hurtled down the hill. Quite a few skied in pairs: an expert father held hands with his beginner child. Nobody fell.

Behind them towering evergreens blocked the sky. Every branch of every tree held its armload of snow, dumping one now and again with a smothering *plop*. The shadows of the great trees were black and blue, like bruises. The wind screamed. The ski lift clattered. Christina took a deep breath to steady herself, and the wind tore the air out of her lungs, leaving her gasping. The patch on her thigh, where she had fallen on the bunny slope had soaked through and was now ice.

"You go first," said Dolly.

Gentle Deer seemed miles long. Bumps and dips made the skiers fly into the air. By the time they reached the bottom the skiers were as tiny and indistinguishable as little colored Legos. "I can't," said Christina. Her lips were chapped, and her hands ached.

"Sure you can," said the attendant, and he gave first Dolly and then Christina a push.

Dolly screamed, knees bent not for style but folding up to stay alive. Christina knew the meaning of "heart in mouth." Her whole insides lurched. The world seemed to slam into her face, speeding toward her as she rushed through it, but she hit nothing. She passed Dolly, she hurtled forward, thinking, How do I stop? I'll go through the building; I'll have a face full of logs.

She and Dolly were caught by their instructor. "Great work! You two are naturals. Not a twitch of nerves. Well, enjoy your day! Keep in touch."

Gentle Deer was boring. Christina knew its rises and falls and was accustomed to the speed. She wanted to try Running Deer. She had become good in a short time, and she knew why: she had forced her mind and body to it because otherwise her mind would have been wrapped around Blake.

Blake and Anya had vanished. Christina's heart ached. Her jeans were so cold! How she wished she could be Anya! Or at least be wearing the yellow suit.

Hours had passed. The shadows of the pines and

firs at the top of Gentle Deer stretched halfway down the mountain, and the snow no longer seemed white but blue.

Dolly said, "I'm cold, Chrissie. I'm going in."

"Don't you want to try Running Deer?"

"My feet are killing me," said Dolly. "My ankles are killing me, my back is killing me, my hands are killing me."

"That's pretty bad," said Blake, who was suddenly there, smiling down at them both.

But Dolly did not know Blake, because he had left for boarding school before Dolly arrived from Burning Fog Isle. She thought he was just a cheerful stranger, and she smiled without interest. She was too chilled for a real smile — the corners of her blue lips merely twitched. Taking off her skis, Dolly trudged toward the lodge.

Christina was inches away from him. She had not grown over the winter, but he had. And he was as handsome as she remembered. His cheeks were windburned, and around his eyes were white patches where his sunglasses protected him. "I'm glad to see you," she said formally.

Blake grinned at her.

Christina felt as weak as Dolly. She wanted to fold against him like a baby blanket and be snuggled. "Where's Anya?" she said.

"Same as Dolly. Wiped out. What's the matter with you island girls? No inner strength?" He was laughing.

Christina's inner strength had deserted her the

moment Blake appeared. And when he gave her a hug, she wanted to spend the rest of her life with him.

"You don't want to go in yet, do you?" he said anxiously. "Ski with me, okay?"

"You're too good for me," said Christina. "I haven't even tried Running Deer."

"I'll ski it with you. You can do it fine. I've been watching you. You have a real knack for this. I think skiing is going to be your sport." He took her hand; or rather, his thick glove took her mitten. They seesawed across the snow toward the ski lift. "There was an English assignment; we had to describe something unusual. I wrote about your hair."

Christina trembled. Blake said, "Anya told me the ski suit is yours. Tomorrow you wear it. She doesn't really like skiing. It was sweet of you to give it to her, but I have to say that it hurts my feelings. You two thought I wouldn't like her anymore if she wore old clothes. Clothes don't have anything to do with it. Jeans aren't warm enough, Chrissie."

She fell even deeper in love, that Blake cared whether she was warm enough. She said, "If clothes don't have anything to do with it, why do you care who wears what?"

He laughed. "Clothes have nothing to do with love, but a lot to do with skiing."

They rode on the ski lift together. Where Dolly had taken up no more space than a straw, Blake filled most of the seat. His bulk was comforting.

"I'm not scared now," said Christina. He grinned at her and ruffled the hair that stuck out from under her raggedy cap.

For that ride, there was no age difference, she was not thirteen going on fourteen, and he was not eighteen. They were a handsome boy and a beautiful girl; there was no world but snow and speed and each other.

Jonah had a crush on her, tenth-grade skaters were tempted by her hair, and Blake . . . Blake wanted somebody. And Anya had left; had she run away? Had she drifted into her lost soul so he couldn't reach her?

"Let's ski partners," said Blake.

"How?"

"Like dancers. You stand at my side and I hold your left hand with my left hand, like this." He held their hands in front and his right hand circled her back. "And I hold your right hand at your waist, like this."

Perhaps that's all there is to love, thought Christina. You both have to need it at the same time.

Blake wants to be in love.

Anya is not here.

I could have him.

Chapter 20

She and Blake glided on and on, his hand steadying her waist, while her heart lost its balance. Over the cry of the wind and the pounding of her pulse, Christina heard a giggle.

An enormous man skied past at tremendous speed, his poles digging into the snow, his body low over his knees. His eyes were hidden by bulging goggles; the skin of his face was protected by a cap with holes, only his lips protruding from lumpy knitting. From the thick lips came a sound Christina knew only too well.

Christina lost her balance, but Blake caught her effortlessly and steered her like a little truck.

The creature of the wet suit and the crunching bleacher — *here*?

On Running Deer?

I am safe, thought Christina. But where is Dolly? Where is Anya? They went inside — but to what?

Blake glided to an easy stop and swung Christina around, their skis in a row, so they were looking up the mountains. "Don't you think skiing is the prettiest sport on Earth?" said Blake. He was smiling at the view, not at Christina. "Mountains under snow. Evergreens against sky." He pointed at the slopes, now nearly bare of people. The day's skiers had left an enormous crisscross of slithery tracks, blue with shadow. Three chair lifts rocked in the wind, carrying almost nobody as the dark of evening settled in: the easy one at Gentle Deer, the medium one at Cardinal, and the incredibly high one — its cables silver thread in a blackening sky — that took advanced skiers to Suicide.

"Come on," said Blake. "Let's go down Cardinal."

"Blake," she protested, "I've only been skiing one day."

"Coward."

"I am not!"

"Yes, you are, Christina of the Isle. I'm going to ski with you, and you can do it. Unless you're a scaredy-cat. Come on. Cardinal. With me."

Laughing, he skied away from her. He looked over his shoulder once to make sure she was following. His long, experienced legs slid swiftly over the hard, rutted snow toward the lift for Cardinal. She was so much shorter and hardly knew how to make the skis walk. Slithering around, struggling, she tried to follow him. "Blake!" she called. "Drag me! Come on, be nice!"

The red suit with the silver blaze came to a halt. Giggling, Christina gripped the loose bottom of the jacket, and Blake skied forward, towing her. She had to concentrate just as hard, though, or the fronts of her skis would tangle with the backs of his. Studying the ground and the backs of his boots, she hung on.

They were in luck.

Only one pair ahead of them at the lift.

But then, it was getting dark. The snow fell even harder, like flecks of sand dashed off the beach in a hurricane. She protected her face with her elbow. I wonder how cold I am, thought Christina. I wonder if I have frostbite from wearing wet jeans.

She dropped into the seat next to Blake and leaned on him. He did not tell her to move over. Perhaps he doesn't miss Anya at all, thought Christina, and at the same time her soul was glad, her guilt washed over her as cold as the wind. She had the strange thought that Blake did not smell right. The preppy leather and aftershave smell were not there. She frowned slightly, tilting her head up toward him. The snow flung itself in her face.

How high they were! No other skiers sat on the chairs around them.

Beyond him, she watched the other two chair lifts jerk toward their mountain tops. Both were on her left. But Cardinal was on the middle. She recognized the bunny slope, Gentle Deer, and Running Deer, way, way over there beyond Cardinal. "Blake!" she breathed. "Blake, we're on Suicide! Why did you do that?"

He said nothing.

She looked up.

It was not Blake.

It was the creature of her nightmares: the wet suit, the smell of the sea crushing her behind bleachers. *It was him.*

Christina screamed.

There was no place to go. Nothing protected her: no safety belts, no enclosures. The lift on Suicide jerked. Christina seemed closer to airplanes than Earth.

The thing began giggling, laughing and laughing and laughing and laughing. Christina screamed to match. "Don't touch me! Don't touch me!"

She looked down. This mountain was not Gentle Deer. It was fierce with weapons — rocks and trees, gullies and chasms. It was not called Suicide for nothing. Below her a cliff yawned, its rock face so sheer that no snow could collect on it.

She clawed at his face mask, trying to rip away the goggles, peel off the lumpy knitting, see who this was.

But it shoved her.

And at the same time, it released the metal bar.

Christina rolled off the narrow seat.

Her screams ran like a streamer into the sky. She went out frontwards, saw the snow coming toward her, heard his giggle, heard the chair lift snap forward, having dumped her, all unknowing. From the ground a chorus of screams from every skier sang.

My folder, thought Christina. It is closed forever now.

Chapter 21

Orange.

Everything was orange.

"It's okay, honey," orange people kept saying.

What did she own, who did she know who was bright neon-orange?

"You're all right. It's a miracle." Even their heads were orange.

"We're just going to strap you onto this sled, honey. Don't be scared; we're right with you."

There seemed to be a vast crowd of people. Legs everywhere, bright-colored legs, not just orange, but all colors: blue, green, yellow, red —

Red, thought Christina. The red suit I thought was Blake. It pushed me off the ski lift.

She tried to raise her head, but orange hands pressed her back down onto the sled. "Lie still, honey. You fell into soft snow. You didn't break bones; you didn't suffocate. That was a one in a million fall — we're guessing just bruises, but you lie still until a doctor looks at you."

They were a rescue crew. Over their ski clothes

they wore plastic orange smocks like firemen or highway workers, so they would be visible in any weather. And the colored legs: it was a gathering crowd of skiers at eye level. They were making a great deal of noise. "Why is everybody shouting?" whispered Christina. She was no longer on the mountain. They had moved her off the treacherous ski slope to the cleared area in front of the lodge and were waiting for the ambulance.

"They're pretty glad you're okay," said a rescue worker. "A lot of people saw you fall out of that chair lift. I guess it's everybody's nightmare."

"I didn't fall," said Christina. "I was pushed."

But the rescue worker just knelt beside her and patted her. "You're still shaken up, sweetie," said the woman in a motherly voice. "Nobody pushed you. The metal bar came undone somehow."

"The man in the red suit," protested Christina.

"There was somebody in the lift ahead of you," agreed the rescue people, "but that skier may not even have seen what was happening. At any rate, whoever it was apparently reached the top and skied on down Suicide. We're hoping he'll get in touch with us and let us know what he saw, if anything."

The Shevvingtons were pushing through the crowd to reach Christina.

Blake got there first. "I thought you were right behind me!" he said. "I looked around and no Christina!" He felt her, up and down her ski clothes, as if expecting to find and set any broken bones himself. His face was white as snow. "She was with me!" Blake said to the rescue squad. "I was going to take her down Cardinal, partners. And then she vanished."

"Got on the wrong ski lift," said one man. "We've got signs everywhere. I don't know what else we can do to make it clear that Suicide is very advanced. Imagine a beginner getting on that lift! Didn't you read any of those signs, honey?" he said, angry with Christina.

"I didn't look up," whispered Christina.

"Great," said the rescue worker. "We have a dozen signs, and the kid doesn't bother to read."

"Blake, listen to me. It was that man. The wetsuit man. He's here. In a snow suit. Red. Like yours. I thought he was you."

"I guess she did hit her head," said the woman rescue worker. "Listen to her babble. Let's get her down the mountain right away. Is the ambulance here yet? Is the doctor here?"

Mrs. Shevvington arrived and flung herself down in the snow next to the sled stretcher. "Chrissie, darling," she cried. "Thank goodness you are all right!" She gazed pleadingly up at the orange people. "It's my fault," she cried. "I didn't watch her closely enough. I had no idea she would try anything like that!"

The rescue squad was absolutely shocked. "You mean you think she may have done it on purpose?" one whispered.

"No!" screamed Christina. "Don't listen to her!"

"She is under psychiatric care right now," said Mrs. Shevvington. "I think the name of the ski trail must have stimulated her."

"It did not!" screamed Christina.

Mr. Shevvington stood over her, too. His ski suit looked black in the starlight. He had taken off his cap and goggles to show his distinguished hair. The crowd quieted a little, just as impressed with Mr. Shevvington as all adults always were. What did he have, that in moments he could make them admire him and believe his words? "We were so lucky," he breathed.

The crowd echoed, "You were so lucky!"

Christina felt like biting his ankles. The straps on the stretcher were not fastened down yet, and she jumped up, ready to beat on the Shevvingtons. Blake caught her. "Don't," he whispered. "You're playing into their hands! You have to act sane."

I'm going to kick them until I have kicked them all the way to the cliff, and then I'll kick them over! thought Christina.

Blake held her even tighter. "They want an excuse to lock you up," he breathed in her ear. "Don't give it to them! All these witnesses! Chrissie! Get a grip on yourself. Smile. Be a sweetie."

Once more, thought Christina, they've won. I refuse to believe it. I refuse to believe that I could be shoved off a ski lift, and all these people saw it, and still they think *I'm* the demented one!

Blake hissed, "I love you, Christina. Now save yourself! Do you hear me?"

Christina turned to the rescue squad workers. "I

cannot thank you enough," she said courteously, her clear voice ringing like an island bell in the mountain air. "I can't imagine how I could have been so dumb, getting on the wrong ski lift. I guess I just didn't shut the metal bar all the way closed when I got on. Please forgive me for causing such a stir. I'm perfectly all right. I don't need a doctor or an ambulance."

The squad looked uncertain. Christina was clearly able to stand and walk, but what was this woman implying about Christina's mental state?

But Christina was saved by Dolly, who hurtled through the crowd, her tiny emerald body like a bullet shot from a gun. "Chrissie, Chrissie!" shrieked Dolly. "Are you all right? I saw it from window! But I didn't know it was you up there!"

Dolly flung herself on Christina, and the little girls hugged. The crowd murmured, "Aw, isn't that sweet."

Blake said, "Let's go inside the lodge and get warm now. Chrissie's jeans are soaked through."

"Yes, she needs to get warm," agreed the crowd, as a single person.

Blake half carried, half led Christina up the lodge steps. The Shevvingtons tagged along. Blake was so handsome and debonair; Dolly was so adorable and vividly red and green; Christina was so appealing with her strange hair in the moonlight — nobody saw the Shevvingtons again.

But the price! thought Christina. This was my chance to corner them with the truth!

As if reading her mind, Blake said grimly, "This

was their chance to corner you, Chrissie. You nearly bought it. If you hadn't been paralyzed for life breaking your spine, they'd have locked you up with Val for attempting suicide. On Suicide Trail. It's pretty cute, when you think about it."

Christina remembered Blake's earlier words. *"I love you."*

The heat of his body had been merely warmth when she was cold; the support of his arms had been merely crutches when she was weak.

But now it was love. Christina was dizzy, sick, thrilled with love.

"Don't faint," said Blake, alarmed, half teasing. "Come on, girl of island granite. Be strong."

Dolly did not like tagging after Christina and Blake. She did not like all this attention for Christina when she, Dolly, was there. Dolly held out her arms to Mr. Shevvington. "Carry me!" she demanded in a high, piteous voice, like a kitten. "I'm so trembly after what happened to Chrissie."

Mr. Shevvington scooped her right up. He was tall, and Dolly was very visible snuggling against his shoulder. "Don't worry, little darling," cooed Mr. Shevvington. "You're safe with me."

The crowd sighed with pleasure. "Such a pretty picture," said everybody, tilting their heads like mother birds to watch Dolly being cuddled. Several people took photographs. Blake and Christina went ahead. Slowly the Shevvingtons followed them into the ski lodge.

Inside, a vast fire crackled in the towering two-story stone fireplace. Logs as big as Christina's room at the Inne smouldered in the stone cavity. "Heat," whispered Christina. "I could step right inside the flames to get warm, I'm so cold."

"Sssssshhhh," said Blake urgently. "You want the Shevvingtons to quote you on that?"

"No, but I want to get warm."

"Where's Anya?" said Blake, getting irritable now. "She'll take you up to your room. You need to sit in a hot tub and get some warmth into your bones. And if Anya doesn't help, you'll have to ask Mrs. Shevvington."

A staircase, huge and solid, circled layer on layer above the stones. It was nothing like the tippy fragile forest of white banisters at Schooner Inne. It was made of great planks of oak, sturdy as trees.

Down the stairs came Anya.

She had dressed for dinner: a narrow white wool skirt beneath a delicate, lacy top with a row of tiny ribbons around the throat. Her hair was spun black and her lips were soft and pink. She was as beautiful as a princess, as fragile as glass.

Blake's grip on Christina loosened. His eyes were for Anya and Anya only. Vivid in scarlet pants and jacket, his dark hair windbrushed, his cheeks windburned, Blake crossed the wide room to Anya, and she descended the stair to Blake. Complete in themselves, Blake and Anya touched fingers. Reaching over the banister, Blake guided Anya down the last few steps, and when she reached the bottom and there were no railings between them he took her in his arms and kissed her. Then, synchronized as a single person, they moved across the room to Christina.

I never had you, she thought, grieving. You were always Anya's.

She turned her head away to keep anyone from seeing the pain it caused her. Grow up, she told herself. You wanted Blake to be the rescuer, and he was. You wanted Blake to be a hero, and he is. So stop pretending he can be your boyfriend as well. You're a little girl. Anya is a beautiful woman.

"Blake!" said the Shevvingtons, shocked, setting Dolly down so fast she nearly hit the floor. "What are you doing here, Blake? Why aren't you at boarding school? What is going on, young man?" They tried to be the fierce principal and the harsh teacher, but the ski lodge diluted their power with Blake. He bowed to them mockingly. "What a surprise to meet again," he said. His eyes were exactly the same as theirs: hard, fighting eyes. If they entered a ring — Blake vs. Shevvington — Blake would win.

For Anya he would fight any battle.

Christina ached with cold and exhaustion. But at least the Shevvingtons were beaten. Christina had survived; Anya had Blake.

The rest of the weekend, thought Christina, trying to summon up energy and gladness, we will ski and laugh and party and stay up late. There would be no more accidents — the Shevvingtons can't risk it.

We'll have food sent up to the room, she decided,

having always wanted to order from room service. Perhaps we'll order in the middle of the night. If there's dancing, I'm sure Blake will save one dance for me.

Mrs. Shevvington's little black-hole eyes landed on Christina. Mrs. Shevvington knew when she was beaten. Christina knew that the Shevvingtons would change plans immediately. She did not have the strength to fight back this time. But Blake is here, she thought. Blake will fight for me. So it's all right.

Mrs. Shevvington straightened. "Arthur, dear," she said loudly to her husband, "after this dreadful brush with death, I'm too shaken to stay longer. I simply cannot finish out the ski weekend. My nerves," said Mrs. Shevvington, who had none, "are frayed. Girls, you must pack immediately. Go to your rooms. As soon as Christina is warm and in dry clothing, we'll drive straight home. Tonight."

But now I want the weekend, thought Christina. She did not have enough energy to argue a single syllable. She could hardly stand up without Blake.

Dolly said, "That's very wise, Mrs. Shevvington. Chrissie can hardly stand up. She can sleep in the car."

"I'd rather sleep in the room," Christina mumbled.

Mr. Shevvington picked Christina up this time. Blake was too absorbed by Anya to notice. Dolly frowned with faint jealousy. Christina was too tired to argue.

Anya wilted against Blake. "Home?" she whispered. "Oh, please, no! I just saw him again. Not yet!"

Just as she manages to blossom again, thought Christina, they cut her back.

"Come, Anya," said Mrs. Shevvington. "Come, Christina. Do not dillydally."

"Anya is staying for the weekend," said Blake. "I'll drive her home."

"She most certainly is not staying. I do not give permission," said Mrs. Shevvington.

"Permission," said Blake, "is not yours to give. I am eighteen. I can vote and die for my country. And therefore, I can decide when to drive Anya back to Schooner Inne."

A chill that was not from snow or mountains settled all over Christina's heart. If I go home without Blake or Anya, she thought, if I go back to Schooner Inne and only Dolly is between me and the Shevvingtons . . . that means there is nothing between me and the Shevvingtons.

Mrs. Shevvington stomped her foot, like Dolly having a pout. "Well, I'm not paying for that room," she said spitefully. "Just where do you expect Anya to sleep?"

"I'll get her a room," Blake said.

My folder is not yet closed, thought Christina, whose eyes had closed of their own accord. And I am so close to the truth now that the Shevvingtons cannot wait much longer to be rid of me.

Blake. I need you. You have to come, too. Anya has to come, too.

But she had not spoken aloud. She was thinking it in her sleep. She had fallen asleep right on Mr. Shevvington's shoulder. She knew it and did not know it, wanted to move but slept on.

So they were back early. She slept through the drive back to Schooner Inne, slept through being put to bed upstairs, slept till way into the next day, when Dolly woke her up. "I've had breakfast!" said Dolly impatiently. "Let's go over to Jonah's. They're playing in the ice maze. We have to tell them everything. And I have photographs. One of the people in the ski crowd had a Polaroid, and he gave me photographs. We'll show them to everybody."

"Of me falling?" cried Christina, waking up immediately, thinking, Proof, proof! This is it! A photograph of the man in the red suit — proof that I was pushed, that I was not alone in that chair lift! I'm there, I have it, I won after all, I —

"No, no," said Dolly. "Nobody had a camera out then. Photographs of us rescuing you. See this pretty one of me in Mr. Shevvington's arms? And here's a really nice one of me snuggling down next to your cheek to be sure you're all right."

Christina stared at the cracked plaster on her ceiling. Do I laugh or sob? she thought.

"What do you want for breakfast, Chrissie?" said Dolly. "I'm willing to fix you something."

"I think I'll just chew on my pillow for a while," said Christina.

* * *

Everybody was startled to have Christina and Dolly join them. "But you were going away for a three-day weekend," protested Jonah.

"Did you wear the yellow suit?" cried Mrs. Bergeron. "Did you have a wonderful time? Are you a natural at skiing? I bet you are."

Dolly said importantly, "Christina fell off the ski lift."

"No!" they all screamed. "She didn't! How terrifying! Are you all right, Chrissie? What happened?"

Dolly gave her version of the fall.

Christina did not offer hers. She could just imagine what people would say. *Pull yourself together, Christina; stop telling stories; behave in a socially acceptable manner; do what the Shevvingtons say.*

Jonah said impatiently, "Dolly, shut up. I want to hear what Christina says. You weren't part of it at all."

"I was so!" said Dolly, pulling her lips together in anger. "Look at the photographs of me."

"Nobody cares about photographs of you," said Jonah irritably, brushing her aside. "Christina," he said, "that is so scary." He pulled her away from the rest, so they were standing in a corner of the house that made a sun trap, out of the wind. "Chrissie," he whispered, "was there something more to this than — well — you know — the Shevvingtons? They wouldn't really go that far, would they?"

The rest were screaming, yelling, pushing, and sliding in the ice mazes.

I could be skiing now, Christina thought. With Blake. Going fast, skimming over the top of the world with his hand on my waist. Wearing the lemon-yellow suit. The sun could be over Running Deer instead of this boring old backyard.

She wanted to share with Blake, not Jonah! She wanted Blake to care, not Jonah! Jonah was just another seventh-grader. Blake was man, handsome and strong and —

and Anya's.

Christina sighed. She said, "I don't know. Let's play."

When it was time to go home, she could not find Dolly.

She shrugged. Dolly never stayed unless she was the center of attention. Dolly had doubtless gone on home herself.

Chapter 22

But Dolly was not at Schooner Inne.

The sun set. The sky went black. The snow began. And Dolly did not come home. There were no little sixth-grade friends to phone to see if she was at their house . . . Dolly had no friends.

Michael, Benjamin, and Christina put on coats and boots and went to look for Dolly. They searched between Jonah's house and Schooner Inne. The snow came down thick and heavy. Hedges turned into white snakes, parked cars became white monsters. Michael brushed snow off fire hydrants and garbage cans, as if he thought his little sister had frozen upright at the side of the road.

"When we get home," said Michael loudly, "we'll find her with Mrs. Shevvington in the kitchen."

Or has Dolly already been in the kitchen with Mrs. Shevvington? thought Christina. Is she missing because the Shevvingtons decided she would be?

"Or she was home all along," said Benjamin. "Hidden in some corner reading a book."

They liked that idea. The island children ran back

to Schooner Inne. They searched Dolly's and Anya's room. They went into the closets and up into the cupola. They looked in Christina's room and under the piles of extra blankets. They went through each guest room, and then the formal rooms downstairs.

Dolly was not in Schooner Inne.

The boys and Christina stood silently in the kitchen, staring at the Shevvingtons.

Even I, thought Christina — and I know how evil they are — even I am waiting for them to be the grown-ups and fix things.

Mrs. Shevvington did not make supper. Mr. Shevvington walked between the back and front doors, opening them, looking around for Dolly. Snow whipped into miniature drifts inside each door.

"Maybe we should call our parents and let them know," said Benj.

Mr. Shevvington said there was no point worrying them yet.

The snow came down. The temperature dropped. The wind howled.

Christina had thought Dolly was pouting because nobody had cared about her photographs and everybody put Christina first. But Dolly could only pout in front of people: Dolly needed an audience for everything she did. Where could Dolly be — by choice — without a companion or a crowd?

At nine o'clock Michael said, "Maybe we should call the police."

Mr. Shevvington hesitated. So Michael picked up the phone and called them himself.

They came, asked their questions, and looked through the house themselves, from cupola to cellar. No Dolly. They looked in the Shevvingtons' cars, in case she had fallen asleep in one of them. Then they said most likely Dolly had finished her hot chocolate at Jonah's, felt sleepy, and crept into some corner right there and fallen asleep. Off drove the police to search Jonah's house. It was such a logical, cozy explanation that for a whole half hour Christina felt good: surely Dolly was safe at Jonah's.

But she was not.

The police came back to Schooner Inne. They wanted a good photograph of Dolly.

Outside the snow fell harder. Is she cold? thought Christina. Is she scared? Is she lonely? Is she hungry?

It's my fault, thought Christina. I should have let her keep the spotlight. I know she can't live without it.

Her words rang in her head. Can't live, can't live, can't live.

"Had Dolly been having trouble at school?" asked the police. "Would she have run away?"

But how could Dolly run away? In a village with no bus, train, or taxi? The only place Dolly would go for refuge was Burning Fog Isle, and no boats were on the water in this weather.

"Like many island children," said Mr. Shevvington sadly, "Dolly had a hard time in school. She was an unhappy little girl." He managed to imply that it had been immoral of the Jayes to bring up their sons and daughter on Burning Fog Isle. He managed to imply that he and his wife, however, had been doing all they could to cure Dolly of her island upbringing.

"Dolly was not liked," added Mr. Shevvington. "Her locker was defaced. Her notebooks torn. The sneakers she left in her gym locker were shredded. A child shunned like that, I'm afraid, might reach for a grim and final solution."

"You're making that up," said Christina sharply. "That never happened. If those things had happened, Dolly would have told me."

"She didn't tell us much," said Michael, fighting tears. "She mostly confided in Mrs. Shevvington. Mrs. Shevvington was really her best friend," he told the police.

Mrs. Shevvington smiled pityingly. "It's a sad thing when a little girl's best friend is a strange grown-up, officer. But it is not unusual for unhappy children to seek out the most stable adult. I think you know the recent history of Anya and Christina. What examples to have set for you! Stability is not an island product." Mrs. Shevvington shook her oat-meal face back and forth. "Poor little Dolly. Perhaps in the morning . . . you should . . . drag the pond. Christina made her go there. Poor little Dolly was always drawn back."

"She was not!" cried Christina. "It wasn't like that."

They will redecorate that guest room, thought Christina. The one that was black and cream, lace and gauze, the one that was Anya. They will make it a room of Dolly. Emerald green and full of books.

Mrs. Shevvington began to cry noisily. Her crying was as ugly and solid as her face. Mr. Shevvington put an arm around her to comfort her.

The police officer said quickly, "Nobody blames you. You did your best. Anything could have happened. Going to a friend's house without calling you. Falling through thin ice."

Nobody would blame the Shevvingtons.

Why, the Shevvingtons would act as horrified as anybody. They would weep in front of people, saying it was their fault. People would gather around to reassure them. "It wasn't your fault," they would tell Mr. and Mrs. Shevvington, adding in a whisper, "Those island girls . . . so unstable . . . so strange. In the end, Dolly was no different."

If Christina told the police that Evil stood before them, fixing coffee, they would say Christina had gone winter mad. If Christina said, "Guess what almost happened to me skiing," the police would say to the Shevvingtons, "You people really have all the loonies living here, don't you?"

"Also," said Mrs. Shevvington, "the island children, especially Dolly, are fascinated by the fact that exactly one hundred years ago, the wife of the sea captain who built this house flung herself to her death by leaping off the cupola onto the rocks. Dolly asked for the details. I thought it was historical interest, and I encouraged it." Here Mrs. Shevvington wept a little. "But perhaps Dolly was planning to do the same. Oh dear, oh dear, oh dear," sobbed Mrs. Shevvington.

"My sister wouldn't do that," said Benjamin. He

was as stolid and unemotional as ever. "My sister is afraid of heights," he said. "She was afraid of that ski weekend because she'd have to go downhill face first." Then he said, "I'm going back out to look for my sister again."

"But where?" cried Mrs. Shevvington. "Where haven't you looked already?"

Benjamin shrugged. "I can't do *nothing*." He turned to the police. "She'd go to the island if she were going anywhere. Let's check every boat in the harbor. She might have sneaked aboard a fishing vessel."

The police thought that was logical. They said Michael and Benj could come with them for the hunt. "Me, too!" cried Christina.

"You're too little," said Michael. "And she's our sister."

Christina was alone in the mansion with the Shevvingtons.

They smiled at her.

Her skin crawled. She could feel the three colors of her hair separating and shivering. She smiled back.

Mr. Shevvington said, "I will telephone the Jayes now."

"Now when you know they can't come," said Christina. "You know they'll have to wait for dawn. Nobody can take a boat to the mainland at night during a snowstorm. So you know they'll sit awake all night, weeping and terrified."

Mr. Shevvington smiled.

Mrs. Shevvington smiled.

She could not sit in the room with them. Their smiles were too horrible, full of holes and yellow teeth and knowledge.

Christina went up the curling stairs to her cold little room.

She turned on the electric blanket and wrapped it around herself, mummy style. The Shevvingtons can't hurt me tonight, she thought. It's not reasonable, not when the whole police force will be back shortly. So I must stay calm and think. Either Dolly is hiding from the Shevvingtons . . . *or the Shevvingtons are hiding Dolly.*

Could they hide Dolly at Schooner Inne?

Christina had often wondered if the giggle who lived in the cellar came up for meals; if when she was asleep on the third floor, the giggle crept up to sit in the chair where Christina sat for supper; to drink from the glass Christina liked; to eat the leftovers Christina had wrapped in aluminum foil and put in the refrigerator.

Now she knew the giggle could ski.

But did she know where he was? Ski resort? School gym? Or back here? With Dolly?

Chapter 23

At two in the morning the policemen brought Michael and Benjamin back with the order to get some rest. They had found no trace of Dolly.

The boys went upstairs. The Shevvingtons followed. The Shevvingtons entered their room on the second floor. Michael and Benj continued up to the third. Christina rushed out to hear the news.

"She's got to be all right!" said Benjamin desperately. "What could have happened to her? She's so cautious."

Michael said, "Remember Anya this fall? How over and over she said the sea wanted one of us?"

How could they forget Anya, in her white gown, hidden by the cloud of her own hair, like an ancient prophetess, murmuring, "The sea wants one of us"?

"I'm calling Anya," said Benj thickly, turning, pounding back down the stairs. Michael and Christina thudded after him. He dialed the ski resort, and over the phone lines, across the miles, they heard the terror of being wakened by a phone call in the middle of the night. "Dolly's missing?" cried

Anya, her voice breaking and cracking like old ice. "Not Dolly! We're coming, Blake and I; we'll drive as fast as we can."

"There's no point," said Benj. "I just wanted to know if you had Dolly, or if she had come to you or talked to you." He hung up almost with violence, frustrated by another dead end.

They trudged back up the stairs. The endless circling stairs, like an endless circling nightmare. "Benj," said Christina, "do you think that the Shevvingtons — "

"Chrissie!" snapped Benjamin, "you're as crazy as Anya these days. Dolly's just — I don't know — lost or something." His voice broke. Benjamin, too, was lost.

The Shevvingtons will have captured us all, thought Christina.

She shut the door to her room. Michael and Benj's shut, and down below, the Shevvingtons' door closed with a *snap*.

Christina looked out the window into the village. In spite of the heavy snow, she could see far more lights than the night she had walked alone to break into the high school. Rotating red-and-blue lights on police cars looking for Dolly Jaye.

She isn't out there, thought Christina.

Christina was wearing her sweatpants with the jungle parrots. Over it she added an old hooded sweatshirt. She put on two pairs of socks instead of shoes. She checked the batteries of her flashlights. She put one flashlight in the kangaroo pocket

of the sweatshirt and held the other in her hand —
combination weapon and light.

For two hours she sat on her bed watching the
lights go on and off in the town. Mostly they went
off.

It was four in the morning.

If people were going to sleep at all, they would
be asleep now.

Down the stairs crept Christina in her stocking
feet. Nothing creaked to give her away. She
reached the bottom and looked up. No moonlight
filtered through the ice-caked cupola windows. The
banisters rose like bones in the darkness. Nobody's
bedroom door opened. Nobody had seen or heard
her.

Through the hall, into the kitchen. She turned
on no lights. In the dark she found the bolt on the
cellar door. She worked it slowly, controlling the
sound of her own breathing until finally, silently,
she could open the cellar door. At the top of the
stairs, she stood listening.

Silence.

She listened harder and separated the murmur
of the furnace and the tick of the water heater.

She listened harder and found the thump of her
own heart.

Then she turned on the two flashes, pointed them
ahead of her, and tiptoed down into the cellar.

Nothing had changed.

There were old sawhorses and paint cans. Rusting tools and cardboard boxes on shelves.

Into the first room Christina went. She felt the outer stone walls for rocks that moved or drafts that came through cracks. She pushed hard on the inner walls. But there were no hidden rooms where a creature could lie in secret. All the inner walls were moldy paperboard.

Into the second room.

Nothing.

By now the damp in the floor had soaked through both her socks. Her feet were cold and beginning to hurt. This is nothing, Christina told herself. Think how Dolly's feet must feel, wherever she is.

Into the third room.

It contained some cardboard boxes sitting on shelves and a large trunk half hidden by old rusting tools.

The trunk was large.

Large enough to contain —

Christina tapped on the trunk with the flashlight.

It sounded thick and full.

It was not locked.

She opened it easily.

Ruby red and emerald green — like Dolly's hair, Dolly's ski suit — glittered in the shaft of her flashlight. Christina cried out, covering her mouth to stop the noise.

The trunk was full of old, discarded Christmas tree decorations — tarnished bulbs and faded tinsel.

She stuck her hand down through it.

Nothing else was there.

She closed the trunk.

She went into the fourth and final room.

The door creaked behind her.

She whirled, flashing her lights.

Nothing moved.

Her hair prickled.

She crossed the room.

From the room with the trunk came the giggle.

"I knew you were here!" breathed Christina Romney. "I knew when you saw it was me, you would come out."

Her hair of silver and gold gleamed in the half dark.

She left the fourth room. She held flashlights in each hand, like a gunman in a western going for the final shoot-out.

But nobody stood in the door of the room with the trunk.

She stepped toward it. Her breathing seemed louder than blizzards, her heart slamming against her ribs louder than waves against the rocks.

Nothing giggled.

Nothing moved.

She took another step. With her icy foot, she kicked the door open.

Nothing stood behind the door.

Nothing at all stood in the room.

"Dolly!" whispered Christina. "Are you there?"

Around her ankles she felt cold air.

Somewhere a door had opened, or a window. Cold off the sea was sifting through the cellar.

But there were no doors here, nor any windows.

Christina walked into the room with the trunk.

She moved her two lights around the room, and the shadows of the sawhorses and the paint cans and the trunk leaped and dissolved and leaped up again.

The cold air was almost a wind.

Cold as ghosts, thought Christina.

The sea captain's wife. Had she come back? Did she consist of cold air?

But Christina did not believe in ghosts. No ghost had tried to crush her in the bleachers.

Now the wind was stronger. It lifted her hair like fingers going for her throat.

Christina walked into the shadows, leaving shadows behind her, making shadows before her.

She could smell the mud flats.

It was the scent of Maine: the scent of low tide, the essence of the sea.

She faced into the scent and followed it, as if it were the smell of chocolate chip cookies at the bakery.

The wall was not the same shape it had been. It had an angle she had not felt when she was in this room before. It now had, in fact, an opening. A passage out to the cliffs.

Legend was correct.

The sea captain had had a reason for building his home on this terrible spot, alone and wind-tormented: private access to Candle Cove. What had he smuggled in or out this grim little rock-bound passage?

It was narrow. The stones on each side were hung with ice.

No wonder the rising tide sounded like advancing cannons when the waves slapped the opening of this passage. But where could the passage come out, except on the exposed ledges and shelves of the cliffs? Nobody could dock a boat there; it was rock, with the most dangerous tides in Maine twice a day.

She could not see the end of the passage.

It was dark out and still snowing.

But wherever the giggle was, and wherever he had Dolly, that, surely, was the end of the passage.

I'll go wake Michael and Benj, she thought. I won't mention the Shevvingtons or the giggle; if I do, they won't listen. I'll say I found a secret room in the cellar. The three of us together will find out what's at the end of the passage.

Christina was filled with the image: herself, Michael, and Benj, standing in a hole in the cliff, Dolly reaching her fragile arms up for rescue. Dolly would tell her brothers about the Shevvingtons, and Christina would be free of the lies they had wrapped around her, from burning clothes to tempting Dolly onto thin ice.

Christina turned to go back out, but her cold-as-lead feet betrayed her. She lost her balance, staggered slightly, and slid into the passage.

She caught herself by taking two steps forward . . . and then she knew the truth. The floor was slanted toward the Cove so the water would run back out. Slick with ice, it was as smooth as the maze in Jonah's backyard. Christina slid and fell. She could not get up. The walls and floor of the passage were solid ice.

Christina slid toward the black unknown. She dug her feet into the floor, but it was glass ice. She dropped first one flashlight and then the other, but freeing her fingers did not give her anything to grip. She braced her feet against one wall, but her weight carried her relentlessly toward the cliff. Inch by inch, she gathered momentum.

This is what happened to Dolly, Christina thought. She didn't jump to her death, like the sea captain's wife. She just slid on through.

I will vanish, too.

My parents will live with the same terror and unending worry that Dolly's will have to. Sympathetic townspeople will deliver casseroles to the Shevvingtons to bolster their spirits in this sad hour. Nobody will ever know. The briefcase will acquire more folders, more photographs, more treasures for the Shevvingtons to look at by night.

Christina fought the ice.

With every kick she slid faster.

Now she could feel the snow on her face.

Now she could almost taste the low tide.

There was a gray ghostliness ahead of her.

It's the end, she thought. Of the tunnel.

And of me.

Chapter 24

She was gathering speed; Christina was her own toboggan now. She shot into the air. She tried to arch, so that her feet, and not her spine, would hit the rocks. But there was no time. She landed with a jolt she felt from the base of her spine to the top of her skull.

She was sitting on a ledge, only a few feet above the mud flats.

With Dolly.

"Chrissie, you scared me," whispered Dolly.

"What are you doing here?" gasped Christina.

"The Shevvingtons' son put me here. Chrissie, when the tide comes in, we'll be swept off the rocks."

"The Shevvingtons' son?" repeated Christina.

"He lives in the cellar, Chrissie. Isn't that terrifying? He's been here all along! He's a crazy person, and he used to be in an institution, but they let him out because the psychiatrists didn't think he was dangerous anymore, and poor Mrs. Shevvington, who loves him — she's such a wonderful person, Chrissie; she just loves anybody, no matter what they do — anyway, she brought him back home. But he only likes dark, hidden places, so he lives in the cellar."

The snow gleamed faintly, as if they were in a ghost cove, near ghost water. Christina shuddered. "But where did he keep you?" she said. The Shevvingtons' son! Now there was a ghastly thought: another generation of them.

"In the passage. We sat there with his hand over my mouth while he giggled to himself," said Dolly. "We heard the police searching. He has a secret door, and they didn't find it. It's thin slabs of rock cemented onto a regular door, Chrissie. Just like in the very best books. The kind I love to read." Dolly shivered. "But I want to read about things, not have them happen."

How were she and Dolly going to get out of here? They could not climb up the cliffs: that would take ropes and picks. They could not get back into the passage; it was iced and anyway, the giggle was in there somewhere. *The Shevvingtons' son!* She knew now that he really would have crushed her up in the bleachers. And that Blake really would have died last autumn if it were not for the tourist who had accidentally happened along. And that she had really been meant to fall onto rocky crags, not soft snow beneath the ski lift.

The Shevvingtons emptied bodies.

Their son tried to kill them.

"How did he get you?" said Christina.

"I came into the kitchen, and he dragged me into the cellar. The Shevvingtons were home, but they didn't hear me screaming. Poor Mrs. Shevvington. This will hurt her so much! She loves her son, and it isn't her fault he's a bad person. I don't blame her for keeping him at home."

"Dolly!" cried Christina. "Can't you see that the Shevvingtons arranged this for you? They heard you screaming and enjoyed it!"

"Don't be ugly," said Dolly.

A giggle interrupted her.

Above them in the rock opening was the Shevvingtons' son, freed from an institution because he was no longer dangerous. "It's him," cried Dolly. She clutched Christina like a monkey, fingers wrapping around her.

High in the sea captain's mansion a window was thrust open, and a light went on. Mr. Shevvington's head emerged. "Mr. Shevvington!" cried Dolly. "Come and save us! We're down here!"

The wet suit began giggling.

Christina knew why he was laughing: the Shevvingtons would save nobody.

"We have to cross the Cove," said Christina, jerking Dolly to her feet. "There are people in those boats over there. If we can get to them, we'll be safe."

"Nobody can cross the Cove!" screamed Dolly, trying to jerk free of Christina. "The tide will come in and sweep us away. And besides, it's all mud flat and salt ice and salt pools we won't see in the night, and we'll fall in and drown!"

The wet suit giggled again and began lowering his dark, rubbery legs, coming down to their ledge.

The Shevvingtons' window closed, the light went off. They were going back to bed. By dawn, when police and parents arrived, there would be a new tide and no trace of two little girls from the Isle.

The wet suit's slippery foot found the first stony step down.

"Run!" Christina ordered, and she leaped off the ledge, dragging Dolly across the treacherous, dark, unknowable Cove. Dolly fought her. The mud sucked on her. Nothing but thin cotton socks were between her skin and whatever lurked in the mud. "Dolly, pick up your feet. Run! Tide's coming!"

At last Dolly obeyed Christina.

She's weak, thought Christina suddenly. I always thought Dolly was strong, like me. We were best friends all our lives, and I thought we were the same. We weren't. Dolly can follow but never lead. She followed Mrs. Shevvington, because Mrs. Shevvington is stronger. Perhaps the most dangerous thing on Earth is the person who always follows. What if you follow the wrong person? The wrong idea?

A whiffling sound filled the air. Like somebody blowing out candles on a birthday cake.

It was the tide.

They would be battered against the cliff walls like small fish; they would be carried out to sea under the water, their hair swirling red and gold beneath the waves.

The tide inched in like pancake batter.

Now and then a tourist died when he kept clamming, not believing a tide could become a twenty-eight foot wall. Picnickers got swept off pretty ledges, where they sat with their potato chips.

"The mud is eating my sneakers," sobbed Dolly.

The water gurgled like a milkshake and came toward them. Christina ran faster, but the mud refused to let her speed up. The water came up her legs, lapping her knees. She could no longer run, only wade.

From the cliff came the happy giggle of the wet suit. Christina looked over her shoulder. He was standing in the passage, waving at them.

The tide began its roar of triumph. The water had seen them and was bounding forward.

Dolly was dead weight, nothing but tears and fear. Dragging her, Christina burst out of the water into a sludge of mud and ice.

The tide screamed in rage and desire.

They were near the boats. If they could pull themselves on board, they would be safe from the tide, for a boat would simply rise with it.

Her ear heard a new sound. A motor. An engine.

Feverish with need, Christina looked up. Were the police here? Had a car pulled into the harbor parking lot?

She had been wrong that the Shevvingtons had gone back to bed.

After all the times she had outwitted them, they would not leave this to chance.

Mr. Shevvington got out of his van.

Chapter 25

But the hands that pulled Christina up were not Mr. Shevvington's.

They were a policeman's. In the wonderful warmth of those big arms, Christina knew she was safe.

"How did you know?" she whispered.

The scream of sirens filled the air. Whirling red-and-blue lights rocketed on police cars.

"It's entirely my fault," cried Mr. Shevvington. "My son is not well, but I thought he could function like a civilized human being. I was wrong. Oh, this is terrible. I am fully, wholly responsible for whatever has happened." Mr. Shevvington told the police that he had never dreamed his son had a way to come and go from Schooner Inne. He had never dreamed that his son would steal poor Dolly.

"He must have been the one who set fire to your clothing, Christina," cried Mr. Shevvington, hitting his head like one who has just found a solution to a terrible problem. "And to think we blamed you! Oh, Chrissie, will you ever forgive me?"

Christina had no intention of forgiving anybody anything. In fact she hoped Michael and Benj were remembering various tortures of yesteryear to inflict upon the Shevvington family.

Up at the top of Breakneck Hill, Mrs. Shevvington coaxed her son to go quietly with the policemen. Giggling, gibbering, in his wet suit, the man climbed into the back of a police car and drove away forever.

It was too cold to stay on the docks. The police rushed the girls into their cars, drove quickly up Breakneck Hill Road and carried them into the Inne, although Christina said it was the last place she wanted to be. "There, now," said the policeman comfortingly. "We took the bad guy away. It's warm in the Inne. And your island friend Anya just got there."

Anya! thought Christina. It will be all right. Anya and Blake are there; I'll have allies, people who understand, safety in numbers.

And sure enough, Blake, whose arms were wrapped around Anya to comfort her, spread his arms wider to hold Christina, too, so he was rocking two girls back and forth. One was granite, one fragile as a tern in a storm, but tonight it was difficult to tell which was which. "I've got you, Anya," murmured Blake. "Everything's all right, Dolly's all right." And to Christina he said, "You're so tough, kid. I love how you're so tough. You can handle anything, but I'm taking Anya to live with my aunt in Portsmouth. She's had enough of this crazy town. She needs a city and a fresh start."

Benjamin and Michael flew down the stairs to

hold their little sister. This lasted about a minute, when brotherly love ran out because the neighbors brought over doughnuts and coffee. Interest in food always ran higher than interest in sisters.

Mouth full of jelly doughnut, Benj, whom Christina had counted on to figure out the truth, said, "Dolly's okay. All's well that ends well. I admire you guys for taking your son back. I'm just sorry that your son never got well."

Christina could not believe it. She wanted to kick him.

"And I'm sorry we didn't believe your stories, Chrissie," said Michael. "All those times I told you to stop yarning — the giggle and the cellar and the clothes — it was all true. This person did it all."

"He didn't do it!" cried Christina. "You still don't understand! Listen to me. For once, listen to me! The Shevvingtons gave him his orders. They planned this. They trained him."

She had lost her audience. They went back to doughnuts.

"I'm going to call all the parents," said the policeman, "to let them know you're safe and everything's fine."

Mrs. Shevvington had managed to turn her oatmeal face into a fairly good replica of a human being, with an expression of grief and shame. "We'll have workmen come and seal up that cliff passage," said Mrs. Shevvington. She shuddered noticeably. "It's so dreadful. I had no idea at all!"

"You were feeding him," said Christina. "You had to have had some idea."

Mrs. Shevvington looked reprovingly at Christina. "We had a little apartment near the harbor for him. We gave him an allowance, Christina. How were we to know he had found a means of sneaking in? We would never have kept innocent children in a house where such things were going on! Really! I am an English teacher. My husband is a high school principal. Children and their dear little lives are our greatest and first concern."

The grown-ups in the room and the three Jaye children all nodded. Even Anya and Blake nodded.

So this is what a scapegoat is, Christina thought. You find somebody to blame it on, and everybody is happy. Even the victims are happy. "I don't believe this," Christina said.

Mr. Shevvington, elegant and citified, looked both strong and hurt, dignified and crushed. "Mrs. Shevvington and I are so proud of you, Christina. And of course, we owe you our apologies."

Christina snorted.

"When I talk to Mommy and Daddy on the phone," said Dolly, "I'm going to ask if I can finish sixth grade on the island. I think I'm too young for the mainland."

Her brothers said she was being brave and sensible. The Shevvingtons said, Oh, how they would miss her!

And, oh, how empty your file will be! thought Christina.

Christina could no longer stand being around any of these people. She went upstairs to take a shower, where gradually she turned the water from lukewarm to boiling. She washed her hair twice till it squeaked and, when she got out, towelled it dry. The gold and silver hair dried more quickly than the chocolate brown, and the gleaming ringlets curled in layers.

Christina went back downstairs. Temper, she said to herself. I must not lose my temper.

Dolly, Michael, and Benj had finished telling their parents everything.

Now the policemen were on the phone to Christina's mother and father. ". . . and your daughter is a heroine. Such presence of mind, such courage. She knew the only hope was to cross the Cove, and she managed it. I bet they'll want to interview her on television. Probably re-enact the whole thing for the cameras."

By now the downstairs was filled with noisy, happy people. It looked, for the first time, the way an inn should: a place where guests came to celebrate. All smiled lovingly at the Shevvingtons. Anya and Blake sat on a sofa, Anya asleep against his shoulder, Blake calm and proud to be the one supporting her. "It takes courage, also, Arthur," said one neighbor, "to admit poor judgment. The town will stand behind you, Arthur. You did what you thought was best."

Christina ate a jelly doughnut in two bites, took the phone from the policeman and shouted, "I saved Dolly, Daddy!"

"We're so proud of you, Chrissie," said her father in a choked voice. "Your mother and I are coming over in the morning. Actually it's nearly dawn now.

We'll see you very soon. Honey, forgive us for our doubts. There really was an explanation for all the things that happened. And now I want you to thank the Shevvingtons for us."

"To do what?" repeated Christina.

"Thank them. When they realized who must have committed the terrible crime of taking Dolly, they telephoned the police right away and admitted the circumstances. What responsible behavior. I think he is the best principal we've ever had."

Far from being tarnished by this, the Shevvingtons would win gold medals!

Mrs. Shevvington was smiling.

Never would Christina Romney thank Mrs. Shevvington for anything.

"Dolly, darling," said Mrs. Shevvington, "let me tuck you into bed. You have had a long and terrible twelve hours."

"First I have to thank my best friend," said Dolly. Almost shyly she approached Christina. The room went silent, watching them. "I'm sorry, Chrissie," she said humbly.

"It doesn't matter," said Christina. Christina kissed Dolly.

It did matter. She did not know if they could be friends again or not.

The Shevvingtons had gotten away with everything.

But I'm alive. Dolly has not been hurt in an accident. Anya is sane . . . well, maybe she's getting there. Blake is back.

I fought a good war.

But I didn't win.

The enemy is still on the battlefield. Still teaching. Still running a school. Still living at Schooner Inne.

Christina had not, after all, brought Val back, nor located Number Six of laughter and gold. Nor produced the files of past Shevvington victories.

Dolly smiled trustingly at Mrs. Shevvington, trustingly took her hand, trustingly followed her up the stairs that swirled like mad white fences.

The Shevvingtons would start again.

It would never end.

Don't miss Losing Christina 3: Fire,
the suspenseful last book in
Caroline B. Cooney's compelling trilogy.

A damp, cold finger touched her neck, and she
screamed, leaping backward.

It was only Robbie. Ordinary old Robbie from
English class. "Robbie, you scared me," she accused
him, panting for breath. "I dropped my purse." Why
am I so jumpy? she thought.

Her scream had drawn attention. A strange, silent, serious attention. Eyes stared at Christina —
and at the ground around her.

On the pavement, where children of another generation had painted hopscotch lines, lay a dozen
books of matches. Her cloth purse was not as fat as
it had been: All those matchbooks had spurted out
when the purse hit the ground.

The principal had been standing on the school
steps, waiting for the warning bell to summon the
children to class. Now Mr. Shevvington walked
down the wide granite slabs, his polished black
shoes clapping like hands against the rock. He was
very tall. Christina had to look way up into his face.
The sun was behind him, flooding her eyes, so she
had to duck her head.

Mrs. Shevvington pointed to the matchbook pile.
"Christina," she said into the listening silence.
"What have you been setting fire to?"

About the Author

Caroline B. Cooney lives in a small seacoast village in Connecticut. She writes every day and then goes for a long walk down the beach to figure out what she's going to write the following day. She's written over fifty books for young people including *The Party's Over*; the acclaimed *The Face on the Milk Carton* quartet; *Flight #116 Is Down*, which won the 1994 Golden Sower Award for Young Adults, the 1995 Rebecca Caudill Young Readers' Book Award, and was selected as an ALA Recommended Book for the Reluctant Young Adult Reader; *Flash Fire*; *Emergency Room*; *The Stranger*; and *Twins*. *Wanted!* and *The Terrorist* were both 1998 ALA Quick Picks for Reluctant Young Adult Readers.

Ms. Cooney reads as much as possible and has three grown children.